The Way of Love

George
— a Gift
Enjoy, Thinking of You.
love Ruth
x

The Way of Love

Nigel Watts

Thorsons
An Imprint of HarperCollins*Publishers*

Thorsons

An Imprint of HarperCollins*Publishers*

77–85 Fulham Palace Road

Hammersmith, London W6 8JB

Published by Thorsons 1999

10 9 8 7 6 5 4 3 2 1

A catalogue record for this book
is available from the British Library

ISBN 0 7225 3773 5

Printed and bound in Great Britain by
Caledonian International Book Manufacturing Ltd, Glasgow

The earth and the sand are burning.
Put your face on the burning sand and
on the earth of the road, since all those
who are wounded by love must have the
imprint on their face, and the scar must
be seen. Let the scar of the heart be seen,
for by their scars are known the men
who are in the way of love.

The Prophet Muhammad

Author's note

The life of Jalal-uddin Rumi, the 13th-century mystic known to the west as 'Rumi', is well documented, and many of the events which follow are taken from biographical sources. I wish to express my indebtedness to his son and first biographer, Sultan Walad; also to the writings of the 14th-century hagiographer Shamsuddin Aflaki. The more recent source books I have used include those of Afzal Iqbal, Mehmet Önder and Annemarie Schimmel; for insight into the Sufi path, the writings of Idries Shah and Irina Tweedie have been particularly helpful – and I offer my thanks to all of them. *The Way of Love*, however, is a novel, and I have taken novelistic liberties: this portrayal is a personal rendering, offered with respect, and the misrepresentations within these pages are mine.

The facts of a person's life are just shadows of what really counts. More important is the light of a person's life. Rumi was incandescent, and his light pours from the words he left behind. More than any other texts, it was his monumental collections of poems which formed the beginning and the end of my research, and I wish to thank their original author and also his translators, most notably R.A.Nicholson, Nevit Oguz Ergin and Coleman Barks. The teaching stories in the novel are Rumi's; however, with the exception of the poems on pages 169 and 186–7, the poems that appear are mine.

I also gratefully acknowledge support from the British Library/Penguin Books Fellowship, and thank Muhammad Isa Waley, Head of Persian and Turkish Collections at the British Library, for his time and readiness to answer my questions.

A glossary is provided at the back of the book to explain foreign terms.

•◆•

Jalal-uddin (literally, 'the grandeur of religion') never recovered from the impact of meeting Shams ('the sun') of Tabriz. In an attempt to convey his spiritual insights he gave rise to many thousands of verses, spontaneously sung aloud and copied down by his followers. Though his later work, the *Mathnawi,* has been likened to the Qur'an in terms of its spiritual significance, he had no great love for his own words: it was only because people demanded words from him that he dealt in them at all. Words, even beautiful and wise ones, may point to God, but none will take you there. We must perform the end of the journey in silence, for the Sufi path is the way of love, and true love is always tongue-tied.

Chapter One

There is a sun within us, so bright and so hot that the merest glimpse will char us to ashes. There are suns too, that walk in the form of people. If the eyes of our hearts were open, we would see them, the smoking footprints they leave, smell the incense of their burning hearts. But such people are rare; rarer still is the sight of them. Few have the eyes to see such a one as Shamsi Tabriz, the Sun of Tabriz.

We are covered up; most of us are cloudy days, the brilliance of our light obscured by rain clouds. We live in a cold and dark country where a watery sun grows pale crops and paler faces. Can we ever believe it will be warm when we have to break the ice on the water pail every morning? In the darkest night, when the slice of moon casts just enough light to show the depth of darkness that surrounds it – can we ever believe there is a world of colour? Look at us – we seem so cold, so blind. The sun is hidden in us; we are pebbles, worthless and smeared with dirt. Cast sunlight on granite, so they say, and a ruby will grow. Likewise, a human being can also be transformed by the light of the inner sun. Listen to the story of such a transformation, the story of Jalal:

•◆•

Jalal-uddin Muhammad din ar-Rumi was a blessed child born into a cradle rocked by two forces: that of God and that of man. On one flank of the cradle were the hands of his father and grandfather: Bala Walad and the sage Husain ibn Ahmad Khatibi, revered servants of God. And on the other flank was the man called Temüjin, now ruler of All the Mongols, given the rank of *khan* and the title of *Chingiz* – 'the ocean'. One man, but with an ocean of soldiers. The Mongol flood had turned aside from China and now was heading westward, seeping over the lands of Persia like water from a burst river. Already Balkh to the north, the childhood home of Jalal, had been drowned, its people floundering in blood. A dream had warned Jalal's father of the city's fate, and he had fled with his family and followers to Anatolia. This land, governed by the Turkish Seljuks, marked the dyke against the advancing tide of bloody conquest. Its capital was the ancient city of Konya, a prosperous place, well guarded by its high walls with ornamented towers and deep moat protecting the twelve gates of the city. But barely three days' ride away the crescent of Islam met the fierce horsemen of the Mongolia. And it was here that Jalal found himself.

Just as a sense of his own mortality can spur a person to action, so the report of another fallen city, another massacre, spurred the people of the fortified capital to prize their fragile jewels ever more. And Jalal was one of their most precious gems. His mind was quick, and he learnt his skills with ease; he was precocious and humble in equal measure. Jurisprudence, religious law, philosophy, linguistics: he excelled in each, drinking his tutors dry, matching the best minds in debate by the time he reached manhood. Konya loved his famous father, and though Jalal had yet to step from behind his shadow, the townspeople came to love his illustrious son too. Riches were offered, and declined, land donated and given away; father and son were as wealthy as they were poor, beyond the reach of need and ambition alike. Jalal trod lightly on the earth, and it was from beneath a beautiful yoke that he pulled the cart of his life.

It was the fifth day of Ramadan when his father's servant called Jalal from the medrese, one of the many religious colleges of Konya. It was a bitter winter, and the old man was propped up on a bolster, a thick shawl round his shoulders, another over his knees. His skin was pallid and his beard, once thick and black, was now yellow. The flesh on his fingers was as loose as a cotton glove. An accounts ledger lay on his lap. 'Your eyes are better than mine. You will check these numbers.'

Jalal did as he was told.

'Is nothing left outstanding?' his father asked when he had finished.

'All debts are paid, all payments received.'

The old man nodded and held his hands out. Jalal offered him the ledger, but his father shook his head irritably. 'No, no, no. The *other* book.'

Jalal guessed his father's meaning, and fetched the Qur'an from the high shelf and unwrapped it from its cloth. He stilled the tremor in the old man's hands with his own fingers and guided the holy book so he could kiss it. Baha Walad made no attempt to open it: there was no need for him to read the words; he was a *hafiz,* one who had memorised the Qur'an: these words were written on his heart.

Jalal laid the book on his father's lap, and studied his face, but the watery gaze of Baha Walad looked over his shoulder. Jalal turned to see the object of his attention, but the old man's blinking eyes were fixed on nothing. Nothing but the coming kingdom of God.

Jalal watched the figure on the palliasse with dread. Baha Walad had become more frail with the advance of winter, as though he was dwindling from nothing more than want of sunlight. He had insisted on continuing the fast through Ramadan, ill though he was, and now he barely had the strength to perform his prayers. Jalal watched his father's dancing fingers on the wooden board of the Qur'an and tried to see the man he had once been. Hard to believe now, but just a few months earlier Baha Walad had been full of vigour. His faith had filled his muscles and bones, pulsed through his beard; he had looked like a prophet when he had spoken in the mosque, his voice seeming to issue from the very walls and floor. None had dared to cross him, child or sage. He was the sultan of scholars, they said, an authority second only to Muhammad. Now his noble head wobbled atop a neck too weak to support it. God had turned him into a querulous baby.

Baha Walad squinted at his son as though he was unsure who he was looking at. 'I will be gone by the festival of *eid ul-fitr.* You will bury me and take my place.' His fingers continued their agitated dance; a life of their own.

Jalal bit his lip to stop himself protesting. How could he die? This was just a passing infirmity, a winter ague which the spring sun would disperse. This nodding head would surely shake itself clear, these wasted muscles grow strong with the return of regular food. Reduced even thus in his body, his father's spirit was still that of a colossus: how could something so massive become nothing?

The room was cold, and Jalal banked up the meagre fire, kneeling before the grate and blowing onto the flames. He took off his cloak and laid it around his father's shoulders, and then knelt by the sleeping pallet and grasped the old man's hand. He massaged it as though he could force life back into its grip. 'You will be all right, father.'

Jalal had seen death before. As a child he had witnessed the Mongol slaughter at Samarqand, watched in horror as buildings burnt, their fleeing inhabitants slashed down by swords. He had seen how swiftly the spirit could be severed from the body; he had walked through the smouldering remains of homes and seen the faces of corpses, their open mouths, arms flung wide as if still in flight. Now it was the turn of Baha Walad.

'I am not ready, father. You cannot leave me now,' he said at last.

The old man unlocked his fingers from his son's and stroked Jalal's hair, his trembling fingers running down his cheek to his chin. He patted his son's beard, and the young man knew that, for a moment, he had his father back. It was such a familiar gesture, this restrained caress, that he let out a sob. Jalal wanted nothing more than to seize this moment, stay here forever with his father brushing his cheek, never to grow up, or grow older, or depart from each other. His grief was distilled in a single tear which rolled down his cheek onto his father's finger.

'Man dies in accordance with the way he lived,' the old

man murmured. 'And he is mustered in accordance with the way he dies. I will die at peace.'

The old man's fingers tightened round his son's beard. 'So strong you have grown, so full of promise.' A smile creased the old man's face. 'Do you remember the words of the great Attar? You were a child when we stayed in Nishapur. And what did he say when he saw you walking behind me? Do you remember?'

Jalal indulged his father one last time. 'I remember, father. He said "Glory be to God. There goes a great river dragging a mighty ocean behind it!"'

'A mighty ocean,' the old man murmured. 'An ocean destined to flood the world.'

Jalal found himself weeping, and he turned his face away. He was ashamed of his grief, embarrassed at what it signalled. True, he was an ocean – an ocean of selfish tears. He did not want to be left alone to face the world.

'You will take my place,' the old man said again. 'The world is full of thirsty people.'

'Thirsty for God?'

Baha Walad laughed weakly, his teeth chattering with cold. 'One or two, perhaps. Most are thirsty for this –' He grasped his son's hand and squeezed as hard as his failing strength would allow, but he was tired, and it amounted to little more than a handshake. 'Friendship. Love. Belonging. An end to pain.' He let his eyelids close, his face suddenly lifeless. 'I will sleep now.'

It was not just protection from his responsibilities that Jalal sought in his father, but protection against far greater forces. Kneeling beside his father on that day, watching the colour drain from his face, he realised that without an interlocutor, he would be face to face with himself; with no hand to hold, he would be face to face with God.

With his fingers wrenched from Baha Walad's grip, they curled into fists and beat at the doors of heaven. That night Jalal cursed his maker, and wept in contrition for his rebelliousness, only to curse again. He prostrated himself, praying for so long that his beard, wet with tears, froze to the ground. And still his father died.

•◆•

For forty days after Baha Walad's passing, the city was in mourning. The sultan and his emirs did not ride their horses, a pall was cast over the feasting of *eid ul-fitr,* which marked the end of the long fast at Ramadan. Jalal was inconsolable. Kerra Hatun, his young wife, wept more for her husband, and later for herself, than for the death of her father-in-law. Though she had tried to love him, Baha Walad had always intimidated her with his severe looks and his religious observances. And anyway, there was no need to shed tears on his behalf: he had lived a long and pious life; he was a good man who was standing now before Allah. It was Jalal who was the focus of her concern. The man whom she loved so much had gone, and in his place was an ashen-faced impostor. *This* was not her husband; he was a charmed young man whose life had been as smooth as his brow, a man quick to laugh and slow to anger. Now every effort she made to distract him was met with blank looks and irritability. When she saw the way he looked at their two sons, happy boys who had no patience for grief, and saw the gulf this death had opened up she wrung her hands and wept bitter tears.

'Where have you gone, husband?' she cried, seizing his robe and shaking him.

He made no attempt to defend himself. 'I have nobody in the world now,' he told her. 'I am alone.'

'Am I not your wife still?'

'My wife, yes, but not my friend.'

She pushed him away and snatched the poker from the grate. Jalal thought she would hit him with it, but she stoked the fire angrily, stabbing at a charred log so it sprayed sparks into the room. Jalal watched the pinpoints of lights as though they were just sparks, and not the signs of his wife's spitting anger.

'How was your father your friend?' she asked, her voice as sharp as broken glass. 'When you weren't frightened of him, you were in awe of him.'

Jalal did not answer. If Kerra could have understood she would not have asked the question. No answer he gave would mean anything to her.

But what did he mean by calling his father a friend? She was right: Baha Walad was a formidable man who scared not only his son, but many others too. He wore his greatness like a cloak, impossible to ignore. But in spite of his sharp glance and unsmiling countenance, Baha Walad was as soft and skittish a lover as any young girl. The object of his devotion? God. Baha Walad, like his son, was born into a family whose allegiance ran deeper than any blood tie: he was a member of the family of the lovers of God. And each member of the family, regardless of age or station or tribe, was friend to the other.

Jalal ordered that they take his father's rooms in the college: two simple cells of sun-baked bricks, wooden palettes for beds. Kerra, as he knew, would be provoked by this.

'Where are the comforts due to you?' she complained. 'Why, when your station soars, does our comfort plummet?' She sent out servants to fetch their silver and fine carpets, but Jalal forbade them to be brought to this new home.

'Childhood is over, wife,' he said. 'We must leave our playthings behind. My father is dead, I am his successor and you are my wife. We will live well, *insh'allah,* and serve both God and the people.'

'And our children – are you to deny them their childhood? Should they become beggars and old men?'

Jalal lifted the covering from the window and beckoned to his wife. There had been a blizzard in the night, and snow lay over the streets and roofs of the city. Both were caught at the sudden beauty of the sight. 'Call our children,' he told his wife.

'Sultan Walad! Alaeddin!'

The two boys came running and sliding towards them. This was the first snow that either boy had seen, and they were barely contained in their delight. Swaddled against the cold, the boys did indeed look like two red-faced, fat old men. Jalal reached down to touch their heads, and they laughed for the sheer joy of seeing their father smile.

'To become an old man such as these is the goal of my life,' he told Kerra.

She turned from the window so the boys did not see her tears. The rare glimpse of Jalal's sun from behind such storm clouds served only to remind her how deep and how long the winter was to be. Kerra knew that Baha Walad's death was as necessary to Jalal – and as painful – as the splitting of a nut is necessary to its germination. For as long as his father was alive, Jalal would never have to step from behind the protection of his cloak. No man fully achieves his maturity until his father is dead; and no son of one so great as Baha Walad could live a life fully his own until he had buried the man whose name he carried. With Baha Walad gone, Jalal would be nakedly himself. There would be no intermediary between himself and the people of Konya. With his father crossing the last threshold, Jalal would suddenly become the sheikh, responsible for the guidance of thousands.

Kerra knew it was God's will that the seed of Jalal's soul should swell until the tree of his life stood above that of his father, and she hated God for that knowledge. She wanted back the dark-eyed youth she had married. She wanted back the husband who touched her children's heads and made them laugh. She did not want this man to grow great and distant.

Jalal called his friend Husam to his quarters. 'What am I to do? My father's chair is empty. How am I to fill it?'

'You cannot be your father, but you can be yourself,' his friend counselled. 'Why are you worried? You are the most respected son of Konya.'

'But I know nothing.'

'There is none in Konya who knows more than you.'

'I am still an apprentice.'

Husam turned away from him, and his friend seized his sleeve. 'I will go to Damascus – seek a sheikh there who can complete my education.'

'But your place is *here*.'

'He who has no sheikh, his sheikh is Satan. If I stay here I will surely err.'

'*Err?* And what will befall the people of Konya?'

Jalal was shocked at his friend's passion. 'Why so angry, Husam-uddin?'

'Why so afraid, Jalal-uddin?'

He could not answer.

Chapter One

On the forty-first day, when the official period of mourning was over, Jalal opened his door to a crowd. He looked at the people clamouring for guidance, looked into their eager eyes, and he felt his resolve strengthen. Easier to accept their nomination, take his father's chair at the medrese, preach sermons, pronounce on disputes, pen petitions, than to do what he was about to do, but his path was plainly laid before him. Not for him the well trodden route of the book-bound imam; everything that his father had taught him was in preparation for this moment of choice, and though the path was strewn with obstacles, he took the first step upon it.

He held up his hands to still the crowd. 'I have nothing to teach you,' he said. 'I love the people of Konya, and God willing, one day I will be a fit successor to my father. Until then, my lips must remain sealed.'

He closed his door and leant against it as though expecting the crowd to force it open.

'What are you doing?' Kerra hissed. 'Are you mad? How will we live if you don't take your father's place at the college?'

'With God's help.'

Though he suddenly quailed at the thought of what he had done, of one thing he was sure: he was not yet ready to be the spiritual guide of these people. He had walked to the parapets of his father's knowledge only to find that there was more and yet more territory beyond. How could he lead people if he was lost himself?

And so he shut himself away with his books, seeking an answer in their pages like a desperately lost traveller poring over a map. He refused all company and all diversion. 'He is stricken with grief,' some said. 'Leave him alone, and his wounds will heal.'

'He has not the stature of his father,' others said, 'and he is ashamed.'

'Or afraid.'

'But he has a duty to us,' others countered. 'Whatever his feelings, he should put them aside. Baha Walad was not his only father – we were all fathers to him; we clothed him and fed him and trained him in preparation for this day. Now he must repay that debt.'

Only one man knew Jalal's heart, a stranger to Konya wrapped in a woollen robe. This was Seyyid Burhan.

Chapter Two

Seyyid Burhan had studied at the feet of Jalal's father in Balkh. He showed such promise that Baha Walad took him as a tutor for his young son, and a new kinship quickly formed that delighted both teacher and pupil. Jalal had been quick to learn and Burhan had been a generous tutor, denying the young man neither time nor effort. But, seize the opportunity though he did, Burhan could never give his whole heart to his duties, for he was a dervish, one who lives on the threshold between two worlds: one foot in the material world and the other in the inner universe. Neither drunk nor completely sober, the dervish acts with purpose knowing he is an ant crawling across the face of infinity. He assents to remain in exile in the world, meeting his responsibilities and taking his actions, even while yearning to return home. Burhan remained as his tutor for years, and he came to love Jalal as a son, but the desert was always calling him. Finally he asked Baha Walad to be relieved of his duties.

'Why do you have to go?' he asked his tutor. 'What is there in the desert?'

'God is there.'

'God is everywhere. He is closer to us than our jugular.'

Burhan smiled to hear his student quoting the scriptures back at him. 'There is a time to be with people, and a time to be alone. This is my time for solitude. We will meet again.' He patted Jalal's hand, his heart softened to see such pain in the young man's eyes.

And so he left Balkh to wander the deserts of the east. Few who came across this solitary figure at that time saw anyone other than a man in patched clothes, a stranger who spoke little and slipped away when the noose of friendship was offered to him. For years this lover of God was too restless to settle, and he spun through the desert like a sand eddy, passing over the surface but leaving nothing behind. In time, the dross of Burhan's soul burned away and light began to fall from his hands and feet, and those in need found themselves drawn to him. He did not resist them this time, for the eddy had erased Burhan. There was no ant any more, just the face of infinity. The person who had been called Burhan had died, and in the space opened up by his absence, other people could step inside. It was at this time that he found himself in distant Tirmiz.

One day at the mosque, he leapt to his feet with a cry. 'My sheikh Baha Walad has died! I am needed by his son.' Such was the respect afforded to Burhan that nobody questioned his announcement. The father of Jalal was famed even at this distance, and so prayers were said at the mosque for this sultan of scholars. The next day Burhan retraced his steps back into Anatolia and into the life of his student, Jalal.

Footsore though he was after fifty days of travel, it was to the medrese of Konya that he first went.

Jalal would see nobody. The door of his cell was bolted from within, wooden shutters over the window.

Kerra tried to stop the ragged dervish from disturbing her husband, but Burhan disarmed her with a smile. He rapped on the door. 'What are you doing?'

Silence.

Burhan knocked again, repeating the question.

Eventually a voice came from within. 'Go away!'

'I will when you answer my question.'

'I am reading the holy texts.'

'And when will you have read them enough?'

There was a long pause and then the sound of the bolt being drawn back. Jalal blinked in the sunlight for a moment before he recognised his old tutor.

'Effendi!' he cried, taking the hand of the older man and kissing it fervently. Burhan embraced him, and then held him at arm's length to kiss the tears that streamed down the young man's cheeks. '*Mas'allah, mas'allah,*' he kept repeating. 'Thanks be to God.'

Burhan led the pale and blinking Jalal into the courtyard and then into the medrese. He took him to his father's chair, vacant since his death, and gestured for Jalal to sit.

The young man hesitated. 'I am not ready for this task,' he said.

'I know. God has called me to make you ready.'

Hearing these words, Jalal fell onto his knees and pressed his face to the hem of his teacher's robe. Burhan lifted him to his feet, and indicated the rector's chair. Jalal sat, and now it was the turn of Burhan to kneel. Though Jalal protested, the older man touched his sandals as a sign of respect. And then, until the light faded from the winter sky and they were in darkness, the tutor once again tested the knowledge of his student.

'And what of the mystical path?'

Jalal listed the schools and their histories, the eminent figures and the titles of their writings. A note of distaste entered his voice when he spoke of such things: the practices of such people hardly accorded with the example of the Prophet.

Finally Burhan rose. 'You are almost complete in your studies,' he said. 'You have travelled to the limit of your father's knowledge of theology and the science of God.

The outer landscape is fully mapped,' he said, his face hidden in darkness. 'Now begins the real work – the inner journey.'

For twenty days, and then twenty days more, the sheikh sequestered his student in his cell. Words were forbidden, fasts were undergone. It was arduous for Jalal, as it would be for anyone, and yet he welcomed the pain, the tiredness, even the confusion. He was an urn in the hands of a master potter, he would allow himself to be moulded into whatever shape Burhan wished. But though he tried to push the presentiment away, the knowledge was there: even as he was wet clay between the fingers of his master, he knew there would be a final firing, a roasting in the kiln where he would be alone. Just him and God. He prayed that he would be ready when that moment came.

Finally, Burhan lay before Jalal a collection of writings, bound between wooden boards, the inscription *Ma'arif* stained with ink on the cover.

'You are ready,' he told his student. 'These are the hidden writings of the way, words so potent that only the trained eye can behold them.'

Jalal was eager to feast on the words after such a long famine, but first he asked. 'And the hand that penned them?'

'Your father, Baha Walad,' came the reply.

Jalal fell to reading the familiar calligraphy as though his father himself had returned from the grave, but then he reeled at what he saw. Whose was this vision: these secret yearnings for God, these stripped bare human feelings? These were not the words of a sober mufti. Jalal could barely bring himself to read the script, doubly appalled: the sentiments themselves were reason enough to give fright, but to think they came from the hand of his adored father!

Burhan kept his student to his task like a horseman training a reluctant steed; again and again reining him in when he shied, easing him forward with caresses one moment and admonitions the next. It was not enough for Jalal to read his father's words silently and to himself, they must be read aloud. The words must be formed, spoken, heard by others.

'This is the inner journey,' Burhan told him, 'the muddying of the feet in the soul. Nothing must be hidden, all must be revealed, all must be accepted.'

Jalal sought an explanation to the text, a commentary, some draught to help the digestion of such unfamiliar food, but Burhan remained silent. All discourse was to be left aside as he felt his way into the mysterious heart of his father's writings.

The *Ma'arif* was finished, and Jalal found his stomach no longer rebelled. Indeed, such rare food served only to increase his appetite. Now, day by day, Burhan gave his still hungry student another morsel from the table of his knowledge, and every day Jalal knelt in prayer, his hands before his face, and gave thanks for his guidance. These hands that had been so empty after his father's death were now filled with those of a second father. Strong hands, loving hands, hands which held an infinity of knowledge.

'But there is more,' Burhan told him. 'You will far surpass my learning. We must travel together, seek out other minds so that you can be completed in a way none other has been.'

•◆•

Jalal was in love. 'He is so noble, so good,' he told his wife. 'He cares for me no less than my father did. I will go with him to the theological schools in Aleppo, find those missing pieces of my training.'

Kerra Hatun was silent.

'Are you not happy for me?' Jalal asked.

'And I? Will I go to Aleppo? Our children too?' She saw the flicker of disappointment in his eyes. 'Or have you forgotten about us?'

'The armies of the khans have reached Kayseri, they say. It is too dangerous to leave the sanctuary of Konya. Here you will be safe behind its thick wall and deep moat.'

'You may be a wise man, ' she said, 'but you are a foolish husband. What life will I have here alone? And if you die on your journey, do you not think I would still rather be with you?'

'You love me so much?'

'As much as you love that man,' she said bitterly.

And so it was decided that Kerra and their two sons, together with a small retinue of servants and fellow students, would form a caravan to follow Burhan into the desert. When it was announced in the medrese that Jalal would leave, the elders tried to dissuade him, citing the dangers, the gamble in such an expedition, his responsibilities to the people of Konya, but they were not likely to succeed where Kerra had not even tried. Jalal was married to the truth, he was a citizen of the search, a father of striving. All other considerations were secondary.

The sultan offered them the protection of the royal guard, but Burhan declined. 'Do you think that if God wanted us to perish, a few soldiers could prevent such a thing? We will place ourselves in the lap of God – we will be safe, or not, according to His will.'

•◆•

Jalal thirsted for knowledge in the way a fish thirsts for water: the more knowledge he drank, the more he needed to drink. He studied day and night with sheikhs and fakirs and dervishes. He discussed the fine points of theology with his friend Husam, and when his friend's eyelids grew heavy, he turned to books until the guttering candle blew out, and he had to rest. His skin, a stranger to sunlight, became pale, and his frame grew gaunt from fasting and penance.

For seven years the small band journeyed through Anatolia and then into Arabia, Kerra following in her husband's footsteps, her love growing just as her two sons grew: strong and straight and healthy.

When entering a new town, even before pitching camp, Jalal and Husam would ask the whereabouts of the holy men. 'Please teach us something,' was their first and only request after paying their respects. Their formal studies of philosophy and religion, jurisprudence and morals now grew to include occult sciences and mystical training of mind and body. More and more Jalal understood the secret writings of his father. He understood now that without the living blood of passion, the body of religion would be a corpse, and a corpse which, in time, would rot.

As the years passed, so visions and ecstasies came more and more to Jalal. Husam witnessed his friend's progress, compared it to his own meagre footsteps, and tried not to envy him. Seyyid Burhan noticed the beginnings of resentment growing within Husam, and took him aside. 'Do not envy Jalal,' he told him. 'We each have a different destiny, and we are each equally loved by God.'

Husam was ashamed to have been discovered, and hung his head. 'What is my destiny, effendi?'

'Your fate is to serve Jalal, just as mine is. Yes,' he said, seeing Husam's surprise, 'we are equally the servant of Jalal. You thought you were his companion, but that is not so. You are *my* companion. Jalal will travel alone for some years yet.'

'What *is* Jalal's fate, master?'

'Jalal is doomed to enter the fire, and burn so brightly that those of us who walk in the dark may have their path illuminated.'

The two sat in silence. Husam realised how foolish it was to compare himself to Jalal. Their destinies were their own, separate and different. Suddenly, in the place of envy, gratitude flourished. To walk beside one such as Jalal, serve him with a master like Burhan, this was a rare privilege.

Burhan looked at the eager pilgrim, saw the changes of emotion that passed over his face, and was reminded of himself as a young man. He was the sparrow who watched the eagle, half in fear, half in awe. Jalal would always be out of reach for the likes of them, and a sudden warmth for Husam spread in his chest. 'These gifts of his have a high price,' Burhan said. 'He will suffer greatly for them. We must love and support him in every way.'

The journey continued, and with each day Jalal scraped more of the rust from the mirror of his heart. But still he yearned for sight of God. Glimpses were all he was afforded, wafts of fragrance on the wind, distant echoes, as edifying as they were maddening. He wanted God in his life as solidly and as tangibly as his beloved sheikh Burhan. He wanted more and more, and yet the way was not open to him.

'What do you wish to know?' he was asked one day by an Atabek dervish.

'God has veiled the truth from us,' Jalal replied. 'And though we may sense the thick covering our human nature has placed over the divine secret, we do not know the names of the veils or their extent. I barely know what I know; how then can I know what I do not know?'

The dervish gasped at the words. He took Jalal's hand, kissed it, and pressed it to his forehead. 'Accept me as a *murid*,' he begged. 'Let me follow you on your travels, and learn at your feet.'

Jalal pulled his hand from the grip of the man, his eyes flashing in alarm. He turned to Burhan, but his mentor would give no advice. Jalal hurried away, but the dervish hurried after him. He ran down an alleyway, but the dervish ran after him. 'Stop, effendi!' the man cried. 'Have mercy on me!'

'I'm not ready, I'm not ready,' Jalal shouted over his shoulder, darting past children, setting chickens flapping and squawking. And thus he was pursued by his destiny.

Though humble by nature and deferential by training, Jalal was often forced to speak his mind when he found shallow men in the guise of imams. He discovered that white beards often hid immaturity of thought, that outward signs of piety could be a disguise for inner corruption. Jalal had seen it many times in the faces of scholars, seen the change as weariness was allowed to overcome exuberance, indolence allowed to replace spiritual hunger. But he knew that all life is movement. If a man became stagnant, he fell into a deep sleep indistinguishable from death. If a man became too set in his ways, he became like a frozen vegetable – black at heart. And so Jalal thanked God daily for the fervour that kept him moving and changing. And daily he prayed for his longing to be increased. He wanted to adore God as he saw his children adore their mother.

Like every good scholar, the more Jalal learnt, the more he realized he knew nothing. Dusty villages, unfamiliar faces, foreign tongues; this was a voyage into bewilderment rather than the certainty that he hoped for. With every passing encounter, Jalal understood more the enormity of his task. Knowledge of God was a great ocean, and his tiny intellect was like a rowing boat: the years he had spent straining at the oars had taken him out into choppy water, but the shoreline was still clearly visible, the horizon no closer.

When Jalal found a man who purported to know, he quizzed him, but the longer he and Husam travelled, the fewer grains of wisdom they found, like two gold panners exhausting a river of its wealth. Now his question was often returned to him as people saw the depth of his understanding. 'Jalal, son of Baha Walad, you have far surpassed us in learning. Please teach *us*.'

Chapter Two

One evening as they were encamped outside Damascus, Kerra went to her husband's tent after the *maghrib* prayer. 'For seven years we have followed you,' she said. 'And it is seven years since my request that I join you on your journey.'

'That is true.'

'We have not died, nor even suffered much from our travels.'

'God is good.'

'And now it is time to go home.'

'Home?' he said the word as though it was a fruit he was tasting for the first time. He paused to judge whether the flavour was one he liked or not. 'Where is our home?' he said at last, still unsure of the taste.

She took him to the rise of a hill and turned with her back to the city. The last rays of the setting sun flushed her face pink. 'Konya,' she said simply.

Jalal did not follow her pointing arm, instead he looked into her face. He noticed for the first time how lined she was, how sunburned her skin had become, how leathery her cheeks were. He had been so busy, chasing the wisps of God through the desert, searching the scrubby vegetation and rocky outcrops for scraps of wisdom, that he had not seen his wife. He had found much, and yet he had searched even more. If it had been a trying time for himself, how much more so for this person, his wife? Rarely had she complained, though she had much cause to;

their two sons knew no different than a lifetime of travelling, but Kerra was a woman for whom such a life could never be part of her nature. He laid his right hand over his heart, his left above his belt, and bowed to her for the first time in his life.

'I will speak to Burhan effendi, and if he agrees, we will return to Konya.'

Chapter Three

'There is one more sheikh for you to meet – a great mufti, a man of broad learning and profound wisdom,' Burhan told his student. 'He will be the final helper on your journey.' He patted Kerra on the back. 'And then we will all go home.'

Burhan led Jalal through the crowded market of Damascus as though he followed an invisible thread. Down narrow alleys, squeezing past camels tethered at the drinking trough, Burhan strode with no hesitation. After so much seclusion Jalal was assailed with the thousand sights and sounds of the streets, and it was only by keeping his eyes on his tutor's rope belt that he kept his mind from being overwhelmed.

They had met many people on the path in the last seven years, but this final meeting was to be unlike any other. For nine days Burhan had made him fast, remain silent and refrain from intimacy with his wife, turning his attention forever inward and upward. Now they were nearing the end of their journey Jalal felt a sudden wave of trepidation. What if this great mufti was like so many others, learned in law, but immature in the way of God? Would it mean that this narrow ledge of learning upon which he stood was the height of spiritual learning, the pinnacle of the mountain he had begun to climb as a child? Yes, the view from here was wider than ever, a panorama of more and more beauty and grace, but there was still a hunger for more, a yearning to climb higher still. He wanted nothing less than an audience with God.

Suddenly a man blocked his way, a beggar holding his hand out for alms. Jalal stepped back in alarm, unaccountably afraid of what he saw. The man's eyes were wild, his strong white teeth clenched as if ready to bite him. His black beard was shot through with grey, his long hair tangled and greasy. On his head was the *kulah* of a dervish, and around his shoulders was a black felt robe, dusty and torn. Tattoos snaked up the beggar's arm like the coils of Idris, the fallen one. The man's hand did not waver, his eyes fixed on Jalal.

Jalal wanted to flee, but Burhan caught his hem. 'Do I need to remind you of the duty of a Muslim to give alms?' he told him.

Jalal held his breath against the smell of the man and untied his purse strings. He did not pause to count the coins, but took the smallest one and held it out. The beggar made no attempt to take the money. Jalal could either drop the coin and let it fall at their feet or return it to his purse, neither of which would be suited to a *murid*, and so he forced it into the man's hand and closed the gnarled fingers over it.

Now the beggar clasped Jalal's hand and then that of Burhan and began to walk them through the market. Jalal tried to loosen his grip, but the pressure of the beggar's grasp increased. It was as though an eagle had him in its talons, the dry skin, the fingernails digging into his palms. Jalal felt as though he could be lifted off the earth, carried away to a mountain top eyrie. Without warning, the man began to sing. His voice was that of a *muezzin*, clear and loud and scaling heights with ease.

I am ore in the fire of God
burning hot until I start to glow,
my molten metal running free.
God is melting, melting, melting
I am no more, not even dross is left.

Jalal's will was no longer his own. He was fully in the power of this man. His arms were no longer under his control, they swung under the command of the man; his legs moved one in front of the other as if in a dream. Jalal was aware of his master Burhan likewise being led, and the three men seemed like one – or none. He was erased; suddenly he saw the body of Jalal as from above, no more substantial than a drawing of a man, and the line that marked his outline did not finish, but continued into the ground, the market stalls, everything around the three figures. A surge of joy convulsed him. Everything, the trestles of curd cheese, the shining mound of aubergines, the spray of water caught in the sun as a woman wetted her bunches of parsley from a brass jug, the kick of dust as a sack of barley slipped from the saddle of a horse; everything, the tinkle of laughter from an upstairs room, the swallows that screamed overhead, ducking for insects, *everything* was charged with joy. A mule brayed, and it was the laugh of God, a dog brushed past Jalal's legs and it was the caress of His hand. Everything was God asking to be seen, smilingly asking to be remembered. Here I am! the fragrance of jasmine called. Here I am! the sun said as it smote the silver buckle of a rich man's shoe. Here I am! Here I am!

The man sang his words, and Jalal heard them as though they were his own words, come from his own mouth:

I submit to the anvil of God,
sweet caresses or cruel hammer blows,

I will thank God whatever His touch.
The beaten gold of a king's crown
the iron in the mouth of a mule,
He can mould me as He wills.
I am nothing, I am no more
Whatever shape He desires, I shall become.
I shall die with joy
I shall melt with ecstasy,
Only this moment of melting is real.

The man was laughing loudly, his teeth flashing. Then he stopped and whispered fiercely into Jalal's ear: 'Use your life well, or I will take it from you!'

It was as though a spinning top had been snatched and spun in the opposite direction. Joy suddenly became terror: the scene before his eyes became vibrant with threat. The beggar grasped Burhan around the waist, lifting him off his feet. Jalal protested at the indignity his teacher was suffering, but the beggar ignored him. Spinning on the spot, his cloak flying behind him, the strange man whirled with Burhan in his arms.

'Stop! Stop! I implore you!' Jalal cried.

As quickly as the man had begun, he halted, letting Burhan down. Suddenly Jalal was back in the mundane world, aware of the stares of the market holders. He steadied his dizzy master, and then turned to berate the beggar, but the man had disappeared into the crowd.

Jalal ran this way and that, but he saw no sign of the man. The market vendors laughed at the frantic searching of the bewildered Jalal, some pointing this way, others pointing that. Finally he returned to Burhan and searched his master's face. Far from the discomfiture he expected to see, there was a smile on his face.

'You are not hurt?'

Burhan laughed. 'Not even my dignity.'

'Who *was* that?'

'That was Shams of Tabriz,' he told Jalal.

'You *know* him?'

Burhan ignored the question. 'People call him Flying Shams.'

'Why do they give him this name?'

'Because he flies like a swallow from town to town, never pausing to rest for more than a day or two in one place.'

Jalal was bothered by this man; not for the impropriety he showed towards his master, nor even for his rags and wild appearance. It was something else that shattered his composure: barely a minute they had spent together, and yet the wild delight that had surged into the scholar's body when they had grasped hands, the intoxication of the sunlight, the sky dancing above their heads, the market stalls groaning with joy – these feelings were unlike anything he had ever experienced. It made no sense; there was no reason for this surge of emotion.

Burhan watched him carefully. 'Our journey is finished. It is time for you to take up your father's mantle at the medrese.'

'But what about our audience with the great mufti?'

'You have just had it.'

•◆•

Sultan Keykubad rode out to meet the caravan when it reached the city walls of Konya. This great conqueror of Anatolia dismounted and tried to kiss Jalal's hand, but Jalal extended his staff as Burhan had told him to do. The sultan hesitated, and the courtiers bristled with indignation. Who was this dusty young man to insist on such respect? Jalal did not lower his eyes from those of the sultan, and the staff did not waver from in front of his face. With a sudden laugh, the sultan drew it to his lips and kissed it. 'You are the king of scholars, and I am the king of countries,' he said. 'Together we will live in peace.'

Sultan Keykubad took the bridle of Jalal's horse, and led the caravan into the city. Jubilant crowds were there to welcome Jalal and his family back home. Konya was no stranger to sheikhs of great standing, but since the sunset of Baha Walad, the sky had become dark. Now, with the return of his illustrious son, the moon had risen over the City of the Companions of God. There was light again.

The sultan wanted to install Jalal in the palace, but he refused. 'Everyone has a place, and mine is in the medrese,' he said. 'Regardless of what my wife thinks.'

So, once more Jalal made his home in the humble cells of the college, and within a short time he began teaching. Words came easily to him, and reports of his eloquent sermons soon spread. Only now did Jalal realize how much he had learnt. He could speak for hours on the smallest matters of law, he could expound all day on a single *ayat* of the Qur'an, following one corridor of thought after another until he had constructed a city of words which nobody other than Burhan could navigate. For they were not Jalal's utterances: he was the mouthpiece only. Behind the words of Jalal were those of his master.

Even though Jalal's scholarship now far exceeded even his father's, he still remained the devoted *murid* to his sheikh. They continued their studies together for two more years. Burhan was an old man now, but as his eyes dimmed with age, so a light had grown within him. He saw many things beyond the spectrum of sight, and had he been blind, his way would have still been clear to him. But increasingly the cloak of responsibility lay heavily across the old man's bent back. For nine years he had stayed in the dungeon of the world while his soul ached again for freedom. One day he visited Jalal in his living quarters.

'My son, I have taught you everything that I know. I have led you along the path of God, opened many secrets to you, given you all the treasures that my teacher bestowed on me. Now you are a lion of knowledge, an equal to me. You have many followers, and you are well loved. Now I wish to leave you, for two lions cannot share a single city. My place is in the desert, where my only companion will be God.'

Jalal protested, plucking at the professor's gown that he wore. 'When my father died, I was left alone. Now am I to be alone again?'

The old man embraced his spiritual son. 'The mystical path is strewn with corpses,' the old man said quietly. 'If we are to fly to God, any attachment, no matter how sweet or beautiful, must be cut down with the sword of the mind. You must cut your ties to me, my son, for if two birds are bound together they will not be able to fly, even though they now have four wings.'

Jalal saw the sacrifice his master had made for him, holding back his own flight to God on his behalf. He kissed the old man's hands and then touched them against his forehead. 'The pain of losing you is great, my beloved *Pir,* but the pain of refusing your request will be greater. You are my master, now and forever. I am your slave, your footstool.'

Jalal last saw his master at the gates of the city, tears shattering his vision into a million diamonds. A small crowd gathered around their respected imam, alarmed at the weeping man, but he ignored their ministrations. There was nothing to replace the pain in his heart except more pain, no antidote except more poison.

Burhan mounted his horse and Jalal kissed his knees for the last time.

'Fear not,' the old man said. 'You will not be alone. A great friend will come to you, a mirror to yourself. You will marvel at your own reflection, and the world will stand in awe of your love.'

With these words, he tugged the horse's reins, and wheeled round, once, twice, and then set out towards the east.

Chapter Four

On his own once more, Jalal threw himself into his teaching, and with each passing year his following grew even larger. His passionate sermons and tolerant attitude attracted many from the poor quarters of Konya. Farmers, leather workers, labourers – all were welcome, none turned away. Jalal spoke openly, criticising the ways of those who strayed from the path – even if it was the sultan and his ministers. The wealthy patrons who sought salvation by donating to the medreses had their money returned. 'God cannot be bribed, nor can my silence be bought,' Jalal told them. 'If I see wickedness, I will speak out.'

He saw beyond the veils of social position to the heart of people, loving them not for their public acts of piety, or deep learning, or for the power they held over others, but for the tiny flame of divinity that flickered within the heart of each one.

Though some of his followers privately protested, Jalal allowed Jews and Christians to come to listen at the medrese. 'The seventy-two religions in the world do not really exist,' he told his detractors. 'Every creed and sect is one. Truth and lies, good and evil, knowledge and learning and piety and faith – these are all one regardless of the form.'

The flame was always there, regardless of age or station, though some people sought to hide theirs – or even to deny its existence. Jalal admonished such people, and soon made no shortage of enemies. But greater by far were the numbers who flocked to hear him speak and receive his blessing. It was the flame that he loved, and where he found it, he celebrated it, whether it be in children or beggars or princes.

Soon his disciples outnumbered even those of his father. Jalal had intended none of this, and as the numbers swelled, so his disquiet grew. 'I know less than they think,' he would tell Husam. 'Why do they gaze at me with such longing? Don't they know I am just a man?'

As his father had done with him, so Jalal gave particular attention to his two sons, Sultan Walad and Alaeddin. From birth they had been like two prized horses, groomed with special care, given the choicest oats and cleanest stables. Jalal's dearest wish for them was that one, or both, would succeed him as imam. But as the boys grew from childhood into young men, so it was clear how different they were. Sultan Walad, a year older than his brother, was a good student, mild mannered, and already with the spark of God in his eye. But though Alaeddin was quick to learn the outer form of theology, he would never know the inner world. He had no patience for prayers; mystical discourse drove him to distraction. When his father and brother spoke of God he struggled to understand, when they persisted, he became irritable. They were brothers, but sons of different parents. Sultan Walad was his father's son, Alaeddin was like his mother. Sultan Walad was a white mare, easily led and placid; Alaeddin was a stallion that would always be wary of bit and tackle. Though the younger son loved his father passionately, he would never follow in his footsteps.

Jalal still accepted none of the gifts that were brought to him, despite the complaints from his wife and sons, living solely on the small payments for the issuing of *fatwa.* He looked at the gold coins that devout merchants tried to give him as though unsure of their usage.

'But how can we pay you?' they would ask. 'You give us so much.'

'Then love God.'

Even though Kerra Hatun worried for his health, Jalal refused the rich food every time it was sent on silver platters from the palace, instead ordering it to be taken to the poor quarters of the town. He lived only on a diet of yoghurt and onions.

'Gabriel's strength was not from the kitchen,' he told his wife. She tried coaxing him with tasty food of her own making, but he ate distractedly, hardly aware of what he put in his mouth. Indeed, if food and drink were not in front of him, he would go for days before attributing the gnawing sensation in his belly to hunger. It was not self-denial that caused Jalal to look so gaunt, but self-forgetfulness. It was not spiritual pride that caused him to let gold and silver slip through his fingers, it was because he could no longer understand the meaning of ownership. Why try to own anything when everything is yours already? Why fill your larder when you have the key to the food store?

One day the sultan sent him a sleek Arabian stallion. Jalal admired the animal, and then laughed like a child when it was suggested he ride it.

'Take it back to the palace,' he told the groom.

'Stop!' Kerra cried. She gestured for Jalal to step away from the onlookers. 'This is just arrogant pride!' she hissed to him. 'You are a man, just like every other man.' Even as the words left her mouth, she knew they weren't true, but she was angry.

Jalal said nothing. He wished it was that simple, that he could return to the days when his appetites gave him pleasure, when flattery and gifts meant something, but every day his desires fell away, burnt from the inside by a growing flame, a single desire – to be with God. The horse pawed the ground as though impatient for a decision to be made.

'I am not a saint, Jalal. I have feelings,' Kerra said bitterly. 'But you just don't care about them. You don't care about *me*.'

Jalal searched his soul to examine the evidence. True, he did not care much for her feelings, but neither did he care much for his own. It wasn't true, however, that he didn't care about *her*. More precious than his own life, she was the oasis of his desert, the pure water without which he would be parched. He knew what Kerra had endured for his sake, the years of hardship, of uncertainty, of bending her will to suit his. Would that he could change his nature to please his wife, would that God had granted him a face more like other men's.

'You are my wife, and I care for you as my wife. I will remedy my actions,' he said.

'Then try to conform.'

'In what way?'

'You must ride as befits your status,' she said. 'You are a sheikh now, a man of prestige and position – not a beggar.'

He called the horse to him and leant his cheek against its neck, murmuring soft words to it. The horse's ears pricked, and it gazed through the gateway as though oblivious of the man by his neck, but anyone who knew the language of horses knew he was listening. Jalal raised one leg to the stirrup, but then changed his mind. He slapped the flank of the stallion and clicked his tongue, causing it to walk forward, through the gateway and into the street. The groom ran after the horse, catching at its bridle, but Jalal told him to leave it.

'I will walk on the earth where I belong,' he said. 'Only a corpse on its way to a funeral is carried on the shoulders of others.'

•◆•

It was only in the mosque or the medrese that Jalal could become who he truly was: a lover of God before anything. Standing before the assembled people, seeing their upturned faces that looked not at him, but beyond him to the portals of the Garden, he could loosen his tongue, and pour – hour after hour – words, and more words. *This* was his calling, *this* his home, *this* his food and drink.

Jalal found increasing comfort in his professor's chair, and when the people of Konya expressed their love for him he was glad. Now when he preached at the Friday mosque the streets of Konya emptied. They began to call him *Mevlana* – Our Master – and though he sought to shrug off the title, it cleaved to him. He *was* the master of the people. And yet all sermons must end, all speech must give way to silence, and even the most assiduous listener wearies in time, and when Jalal lowered his gaze from the ramparts of heaven he found himself as he had started – alone.

I have everything, he told himself. Two strong sons, a devoted wife, I have respect of the community, food enough, clothes enough. I have travelled far and learnt much. I have arms and legs and a voice. Why, then, am I still not satisfied?

Jalal needed his teacher's advice, and in his absence, he tried talking to the city worthies, but they only reminded him of his duties, telling him to dismiss his own hunger for the greater nourishment of the people. His pastoral duty was plain: to translate the hidden meanings of the holy books into a form that simple people could understand, to take God from the page and make Him live in the hearts of his listeners.

'Your hunger is of your own making,' Kerra told him. 'Thank God for what you have, and ask for no more.'

Jalal tried to find joy in the dusty path his feet were on. He mimed pleasure when convention bade him do so, enacted delight in the trivia of human life as he saw others do. He ate more, slept more, forced himself to take the gifts others left at his door. He learned to laugh easily and dissemble, act in the way others wanted him to, and so successful was he that nobody knew the cost of the smile on his face.

'Hunger is the human condition,' Kerra told him. 'Do you see others complaining the way you do?'

No, Jalal thought, and that is why I am so lonely. He told nobody how he longed to return to the wilderness, devote his full attention to God. The open spaces of the desert were an oasis to him, the town a desert. The privations of seven years of pilgrimage were nothing compared to these maddening responsibilities. He was a father, a husband, a citizen, an imam. He was in the world, and this was his place, he told himself, and every time he saw the pain and anger in Kerra's eyes, the way his sons kept a formal distance from him, he resolved to spend less time in prayer and more time with them. But when he did so, he became irritable and abstracted, and Kerra would send him to the mosque where he prayed so long that the skin on his forehead became leathery from resting on the prayer mat. I want to be in the world, he prayed to God. I *want* to want to be in the world. This is my place, and my burden – help me bear it. Help me straddle the two worlds: Your world, and the world of gold coins and Arab horses and a wife who loves me more than she loves God.

•◆•

One evening a messenger came to the medrese: Seyyid Burhan had passed into Paradise. 'For the second time he has died,' Jalal said through his tears. 'First he leaves me, now he leaves the world. I will never see him again.'

Chapter Four

Jalal called his closest disciples to him, and declared that they would sit in prayer for the whole night. It had been three years since Seyyid Burhan had left, and as Jalal led the prayers of remembrance, he felt the absence of his teacher no less keenly now than on the first day of their separation. It was as though a warm scarf, so familiar that it had been forgotten, had been plucked away, exposing him to the wintry draught of worldly affairs. Jalal had tried to wrap himself in the robes of his office, seek warmth in the lectures, the sermons, the writing of petitions and issuing of *fatwa*, but they were distractions, briefly taking his attention from the chill across his neck, yet offering no comfort in the still moments between activities.

As he looked at the faces before him, row upon row of good men and women, he realized how much he missed the company of an equal. Even the figure of his closest friend, Husam, was receding into the distance as the shortness of his stride failed to match that of Jalal. He closed his eyes, rocked from side to side, pouring his heart into his prayers of thanksgiving and pleading; thanks offered for the life of a teacher such as Seyyid Burhan, pleading for someone to replace him.

When it was too dark to see the faces in front of him, Jalal called for candles to be brought. When they were lit he saw that half the congregation had slipped away. One or two people slept, the others looked bleary eyed. 'Stay awake, my friends,' he called out. 'What is a little lost sleep for the gain of eternal life? Husam, you are not deserting me?'

Husam shook the sleep from his head and straightened his back. 'No, Jalal. I am with you.'

But as the wax dribbled down the stems of the candles, so sleep descended over the room until the figures were slumped against the walls and the sound of snoring broke through Jalal's reverie.

He opened his eyes and surveyed the sleeping faces. Surrounded by people who loved and respected him, he had never felt so alone. His father Baha Walad had gone, his old teacher Burhan had gone, his disciples slept, and he stood isolated on his spiritual pinnacle. He searched the faces of those in front of him. He loved them all, but none of them knew his inner world.

He silently rose and left the room. The moon was setting, the first hint of dawn in the sky. Jalal walked through the quiet streets and climbed the city walls just as the *muezzin* called. He watched the occasional lamp being lit, one or two figures leaving their homes to go to the mosque. He knew that most people still slept, pretending to their neighbours that they performed the morning prayer in private. Though he had known this for many years, Jalal's heart was still filled with disappointment. These were good people, God-fearing and good hearted, but still they could not find the devotion to pray just five times a day. Was he doomed to be alone forever – even his closest disciples abandoning him in a simple night vigil?

Jalal longed for a companion. He would gladly have embraced a slave had he seen the glint of understanding in their eyes, but he was like the Arab stallion from the emir's stable brought to fodder among donkeys – he would easily outpace any companion, and what joy could there be in such an ill match?

He stooped and took some dust, ritually washing his hands before blowing them clean in preparation for prayer. Turning towards Mecca, he raised his hands to his ears and called 'Allahu akbar'. It was then that he remembered Seyyid Burhan's last words. '*You will not be alone. A great friend will come to you, a mirror of yourself. You will marvel at your own reflection, and the world will stand in awe of your love.*'

'Please, God, that these words come true,' he murmured.

Chapter Five

God would not have created loneliness without its partner, companionship. An ache does not exist without its balm, nor does hunger exist without its fulfilment. The cure to loneliness comes through waiting, for loneliness is but a trick of time: fragments of a single piece are separated by moments only. From Konya to Tabriz – how much separated these two fragments – a thousand years, the blink of an eye? The same heart beat in two breasts, just sixty days journey from each other: Jalal, the Rose of Konya, one half of the heart; Shams, the Perfect One of Tabriz, the other. Two men breathing the air together, praying under the same stars; two men creeping towards each other, swollen rivers reaching towards the same sea.

Shams-uddin Tabrizi, Muhammad son of Ali, son of Melik-dad, Sultan of Mendicants, was a scholar of every science, an alchemist and theologian who had eaten, digested and expelled the holy books, sought wisdom from the tables of others, found none, and so cast himself adrift from Tabriz. He left his home one day, carrying nothing other than his bamboo flute, stepping over the threshold of what was reasonable and comfortable into the raging torrent of his feelings.

He had emptied his cupboards and burned his house for the love of God, watched the flames climb the sky as though they carried his message to heaven: *My life is the quest. I devote myself to You.* There was nothing to do except allow himself to be blown across the face of the world, following not his own will but that of something greater.

He spent his days in prayer and meditation, and with his rags and unkempt look, people thought he was a beggar, but not once did he join the knot of mendicants outside the mosque on Friday, not once did he hold his hands out for alms. He was a Sufi and yet he denied all knowledge of dervishes and *tekiya* and the path of the Friends of God. He had no name other than Shams, no place other than the world. He lived on God's grace and wild figs and desert berries, and when he could fast no longer he worked in the waterwheel gardens of Damascus for a coin or two.

For years he threw himself into the furnace of God, and the more the flames roared, the more he threw himself away. In time he passed beyond ecstasy into sobriety, until he was made of fire. What could be left of a human being after such immolation? Now Shams was as little of this world as a man with a body can be.

And as he wandered the deserts and mountains he discovered he was still not satisfied. As with the young Jalal, the sheikhs and dervishes he talked to could not give him what he wanted, what he *needed.* He needed more. He needed a friend with a heart that was open enough to let him in, a mind so utterly destroyed that it would raise no obstacle to the wisdom he had to impart. And so he searched for one who could bear his presence.

Such burning light, shaded though it was, could not be hidden, and the name of Shams was spoken often enough amid the market place and the mosques. The name *Shamsi-perende* – Flying Shams – was murmured, half in awe, half in disbelief. He was mad, of course, the people said, infatuated with music and whirling dance. Dangerous, too. There was the scent of burning about Shams, and people shied away from him, for the man roared with a flame so fierce the air seemed to crackle around him.

•◆•

One night in the An-Nusayriyah mountains, Shams heard the scraping of a bow across the strings of a kamanja and voices singing, and found a camp fire, its flames dancing into the night sky, the flickering silhouettes of camels and men. It was a caravan bound for Aleppo, hobbled mules and wooden chests of merchandise bound with iron, and muleteers suspicious of the black-eyed figure who came out of the darkness. Shams offered to watch the animals and keep the fire banked up in the night to fend off wolves in exchange for food, but he was driven away by the leader. What protection could a single ragged crazy man offer? But one of the muleteers had studied the face of the dervish, and he took a plate of food and followed Shams into the darkness.

'You are Shams of Tabriz,' the man said. 'I have seen you before. They say you perform miracles.'

Shams glowered at the man, but the muleteer was undeterred. 'Show me a miracle, and I will give you my food.'

'Your need is greater than mine.'

'Then let me fetch you a plate of your own.'

Shams placed his hand on his heart in silent assent, and the man went back to the cooking pot. When he returned, Shams had gone, slipped into the darkness.

It was that night, in the cold forest beneath the diamond shards of stars, the scent of wood smoke in the air, that Shams raised a cry to heaven: 'Am I to be forever alone – a Persian in the land of the infidel Mongol? Lead me to one of your lovers, a person who will love You not from hope or fear, but for the sake of Your beauty so I may join my voice to theirs. Let me not speak a language unknown to others.'

Suddenly an inner voice spoke so clearly that he turned to see its source. 'Seek out your master Rukn-uddin Sanjabi,' the voice said.

Shams walked through the night, and all the next day. He rode bullock carts and waded rivers until a month later he came to the house of his teacher. Rukn Sanjabi was waiting for him in the doorway. 'There is a perfect partner for you,' he said by way of greeting, 'a man whom you will lead into greater and greater mysteries. But are you fit to know his name? This is a great responsibility.'

'Tell me his name, master,' Shams begged, 'and I will be a fit servant.'

'What will you give God in return?'

'I have given Him everything already. Only one thing remains – my head.' Shams raised his hands and addressed the sky. 'Take my life, Allah, but not before showing me the face of my friend.'

And so Rukn Sanjabi gave Shams the name of his quarry. 'Get you to Anatolia, and seek out the son of Baha Walad of Balkh.'

Thus it was that Shams of Tabriz, Flying Shams, flew to Konya. Though he burned with longing to see the face of this perfect partner, he made no enquiries and neither did he seek him out. A lifetime of searching teaches many lessons in patience, and Shams knew enough to wait for the perfect time to act. First he must prepare himself, and then wait for this son of Baha Walad to come to him. And so he found a room in the street of the Sugar Merchants, where he prayed and fasted for twelve days.

When he at last emerged from his room, the landlord, concerned by the appearance of his wild-looking guest, enquired as to his business. Shams was accustomed to the censure of others, and so he pretended to be a rich merchant.

'And you are here to buy...?' the landlord enquired, suspicious of the man's rags.

'A diamond,' Shams said.

'Then you have come to the wrong town, my friend. We have brass here, silver too. Our town is famous for its weavers and goldsmiths. In the market you can buy lapis lazuli, pearls, onyx. But there are no diamonds here.'

Shams was enraged. 'A diamond beyond compare is in your midst, and you only see glass!' At these words, he looked up to see a man in professor's robes on a mule passing by the open gates of the inn. Many people crowded around him, old men and children, women too.

'Tell me sirrah, the name of this man,' Shams demanded. 'Quickly.'

'He is Mevlana Jalal-uddin, son of Baha Walad, may God bless his soul.'

Shams threw back his head and exclaimed. 'This is the diamond I have come to seek!'

Shams followed the crowd as it moved through the narrow streets, the numbers swelling with every alley they passed as people saw the reason for the procession. Public discourse by the celebrated imam was not to be missed. Above the head of the crowd Shams could see the back of Jalal's turban, and it was as though a light shone from its very fabric. Shams knew that if he called out, the young man would hear him and turn round. He knew he could make the mule stumble so Jalal fell from his saddle and into his arms, but he restrained himself. Friends must meet in the antechamber of speech before they walk arm in arm towards the palace of union.

He pushed his way through the crowd until he caught up with the mule. Jalal was lost in thought, clearly unaware of his surroundings. Shams snatched the reins of the mule from the old man who was leading it, causing the animal to stop. The old man began to protest, but the withering glance from Shams was enough to silence him.

'You are Jalal-uddin, son of Baha Walad, sultan of scholars?'

Jalal looked down at Shams, startled at the flashing eyes and desperate look that confronted him. 'I am,' he murmured.

'Tell me, who is the greater of the two – saint Beyazid Bestami or the Prophet Muhammad?'

Jalal spurred the mule forward. 'What kind of question is that? There is no doubt that Muhammad is greater.'

Shams let the old man take the reins from him, and the procession started again. Shams was not finished yet, though. He called after Jalal. 'If Muhammad is the greater then why did he say "I have not known You as I should have", while Beyazid said "Glory be to me! How great is my dignity because I am filled with nothing but God!"'

The mule stopped, and Jalal turned in his saddle. He frowned, trying to remember why this man was suddenly so familiar. Had they met before? Jalal's answer to the question had been automatic, but now he thought carefully. 'Muhammad was still looking for God, never satisfied to rest in his knowledge. Beyazid was lost in God. He thought he had arrived, but there *is* no arriving.'

He clucked his tongue to make the mule move forward, and Shams was again swallowed in the crowd. 'A good answer, Jalal of Rum,' he muttered.

The crowd reached the Karatay college, and inside the blue-tiled dome, Shams took his place at the side of the room and studied the object of his search. Such a young man! And so serious in his robes!

The medrese was vibrant with expectation, hushed voices echoing from the rounded walls. A cloudless sky poured through an aperture in the centre of the domed roof. Directly beneath it lay a shallow pool of water: the looking glass in which the night stars were studied by astronomers.

A disciple laid a number of books on the low table in front of his master, and everybody took their place.

'*Bismillah irrahman irrahim,*' Jalal began. 'In the name of God, the Compassionate, the Merciful.'

Jalal took as the subject of his discourse an *ayat* from the Qur'an: *The word has in fact proved true against most of them but they do not believe.*

The speech of Jalal was as smooth as the sighing of trees, his words were fine without being gaudy, simple without being coarse, and yet to Shams they sounded like the grumbling of a camel. He tried covering his ears, but the sight of that lovely mouth opening and closing infuriated him further. In the end he could stand it no longer.

He rose and pointed at the pile of books that lay before Jalal. 'What is this?' he demanded in a voice rusty with misuse.

Jalal lowered his gaze from the tiled ceiling of the dome to this impertinent stranger. Two disciples, kneeling beside their master started up, ready to throw the beggar out, but Jalal stopped them. Again, Jalal sought to remember where he had seen this stranger before, but all he could see was the ragged robes and the tangled hair. A *malamati,* he concluded – one of a disreputable sect who courted disapprobation as their path to God.

'You wouldn't understand,' he said warily. These people were well known for their sudden and unpredictable outbursts.

Shams growled, half in pain and half in disgust. He pushed his way through the rows of seated listeners ignoring the protests of those whose feet he trod on. A murmur of alarm broke out as he approached the master. The two disciples stepped before Jalal, ready to protect his life at the cost of their own, but Shams stopped at the table of books. He paused, his body shaking with passion. Then taking the books in his arms, he turned and walked towards the pool.

'What is this?' Jalal protested as the stranger stepped into the water, the priceless books beginning to slip from his arms.

'You wouldn't understand,' Shams replied.

'Take care, stranger. In your hands you hold treasures beyond value – gold leaf and parchment are the least of their worth.'

But Shams did not heed him. One by one he dropped the books into the water. There was a roar of outrage from the crowd and three men leapt into the pool and began to wrestle the books from Shams, but a cry from Jalal made them stop.

'I thought this man was mad, now I see it is my followers. This is a holy place, not a market where you can fight and argue.'

The disciples stepped out of the pool, leaving the figure of Shams alone. 'Well spoken, Jalal,' the dervish said. The water was stained with ink from the pages of the books, and already leaves were floating free of their bindings.

Jalal looked at the ruined books and began to weep as he realized how precious these objects were to him. These books he had studied since his youth. These were the ladders to God, individual rungs carved from years of study and penance. This was as close to the abode of God that matter came. If the *Kaabe* existed anywhere outside Mecca, it was in the pages of these noble writings.

The sight of Jalal's tears brought Shams to his senses and his heart softened. 'Which of these is the most precious to you?'

Jalal shook his head, unable to answer.

Shams stooped and took one of the books from the water. 'The *Esraname* which was given to you from the hands of Attar himself?' He handed the book to Jalal.

The imam gasped. The book was dry. Even the dust on the cover was dry.

'Or perhaps the *Ma'arif*, which you studied so thoroughly?'

Jalal silently took the book – also dry.

'A miracle!' someone cried.

One by one the books were brought out of the pool, each as dry as if they had just been taken off the library shelf. Jalal stood transfixed, his eyes on the face of the stranger.

'There are two ways to make a saint,' Shams said. 'The long path –, he indicated the books, 'and the short path.'

Jalal stepped back with a cry. The dervish seemed to be standing in a pool of fire, flames licking round his ankles. The image had gone in an instant.

Jalal looked from the feet of this man, and then into his face. The black eyes of the dervish blazed with an undefined passion. 'What is the name of the short path?' Jalal said at last.

'The Way of Love.'

'And how can I learn to walk that path?'

'Love cannot be learnt.'

Again, the vision of fire. Jalal looked at the faces of the men around him, but none of them saw the flames.

'You are a lamp waiting to be lit,' Shams said. 'I am the flame. It is time to leave these books behind and come with me.'

This was the man Jalal had been waiting for, the sheikh who was to guide him through the final stages of his journey. He stooped to kiss the man's knees, but Shams took his hands. 'There is no sheikh and no murid anymore. We will bend our knees only to God.'

Saying these words, he clasped Jalal to his breast. When the two men separated, their eyes were wet with tears. Jalal's disciples watched in astonishment as the two men walked from the medrese, their arms linked as though they had been fused at the point their bodies touched.

Chapter Six

Jalal trembled as Shams led him into the street. He watched his feet as though they belonged to somebody else, somebody whose mind was not in turmoil, somebody assured of the direction in which he was walking. There were two people walking arm in arm with the grizzled dervish. One feared for his reputation, his sanity, his life. Such speed – the sudden spilling down the steps of the medrese, professor's gown flapping: years of study and careful grooming by his teachers and in the swipe of an arm, this miracle-working dervish had sent him reeling. Gone was his dignity, his bearing, his poise. He wanted one of the crowd who followed them to question him, ask why he was suddenly willing to give everything away. He owned nothing other than his faith and his life, and both he was willing to give away to this stranger.

But Shams was no stranger. Jalal remembered now that he had once before taken his hand in the market of Damascus. That time, he had fought to release himself; now he was ready to return the pressure of the handclasp. He did not understand why, and suddenly he didn't care. For the other person who Inhabited Jalal was on fire. The streets were on fire, the houses, his robes, his sandals. Fire was falling from the sky, each footstep – fire. Something was happening to him, something so great and so glorious that misgivings shrivelled in its inferno. Nothing could stop this movement of his legs, one in front of the other. Even if this was Satan by his side and he was walking into the mouth of hell, Jalal would follow, praising God.

His heart was singing, for his heart knew the journey they were on. They were walking towards the sea, arm in arm, burning a path up the hill to the cliff. Jalal saw now that all his study, all his discipline, all his practise was to lead him to this moment – the point where he stood on the edge of the cliff and looked down onto the rocks of his own destruction. He had always known of the drop, though hidden the knowledge from himself. There was terror and madness in too soon gazing over the edge, but one part of him had always sensed the wind blowing up from the ground, cooling his face and ruffling his hair. Now for the first time he was daring to peer over the edge.

Jalal turned to look at the people following them. He saw their disapproval, their outrage, the ones who had resisted the call of the sea. They had built their houses in the safe leeward side, windows facing the valley. Houses of lathe and mud, houses of stone, palaces, mosques, medreses. Walls thick enough to stop the wind, block the draughts, cut out the sound of crashing surf on the rocks far below. Jalal's ears were filled with a roaring sound – waves or flames, he couldn't tell which.

Burhan had brought him to the edge of this cliff, and now Shams was inviting him to take the next step. This step was one that only he could make, one which could take him a second, or a lifetime. He may never abandon the solid ground he had created for himself. He could stay where he was, a man of achievement, a man respected and loved. He could build his house amongst the others, sit at an open window and gaze at the cormorants diving for fish.

To move forward meant almost certain death. It meant madness. It meant smashing the precious glass object of his learning and station and ownership. All life collapsed into this single moment, the whole of creation waiting for the decision.

'I can't go on,' he cried, but his words were a croak, barely audible. His legs, his whole body was moving to the cliff edge. His heart was crying for release. Jalal watched himself, his body no longer under his own control. A hand was placed in the centre of his back and he felt a wave of joy so intense the man at his side had to steady him. Before he even looked up, Jalal knew that he had stepped. He was falling.

No more words were spoken as Shams closed the cell door behind them. It was sixty days before it opened again.

•◆•

Everything was to change. Where there had been order and routine, there was now discovery, moment after moment. All learning was as nothing, all memory was erased, all theories were mocked. There was no progress, no path, no time. Everything was now, was here.

'I have come to destroy you,' Shams had said as the door of the cell closed, 'and every obstacle of thought and belief. You will die in my arms and only then will you start to live.'

Jalal had experienced nothing like this. Even in his many hours of meditation, his prayer, his remembrance of God, there had never been such ecstasy. Now pain became joy and joy became agony. Jalal was burned away and a new being emerged, a creature with no name, no face beyond the dazzle of light. Again and again he threw himself at Shams, impaling himself on the spikes of the other man's love. Everything – his past, his present, his future – was sacrificed. Every hidden corner was exposed. The Almighty reached into the still pool of Jalal's mind and brought forth wonder after wonder.

Chapter Six

For sixty days – two whole months – Shams and Jalal were sequestered, a mirror looking at a mirror, infinite reflections, each one a veil torn from the face of the One.

•◆•

The students of Jalal were a flock with no shepherd. Their master had often retreated to his cell for meditation, but after one week, two weeks, he would reappear, his eyes distant, his step uncertain. But now there was no answer to their knocking of his door, no sounds from inside other than that of the bamboo flute, the cries of *Allah!* Meals that they left by his shuttered window were untouched for six days out of seven. Both men knew how to fast: the privations that would have killed a normal person were nothing to such as these. But as their time together stretched into weeks, and then into months, so the concern of his followers increased.

One day Kerra could bear the secret of their meeting no longer. Taking a tray of honey cakes as an excuse, she spied on the two men in the small cell, peering through a chink in the door into the dim interior. Her pleasure at seeing her husband was soured by the sight of him kneeling on the floor, resting his head on the lap of Shams. The beggar with the patched cloak had taken her place, and she felt her heart contract with jealousy.

No words were said between the two men, and she thought they were both asleep. Time passed and then she saw the wall opposite them open like a door. The poor woman stifled a cry as she watched passing out of the wall, one by one, six shrouded figures.

There are some things that cannot be said. Even if words were to be found, divine law prevents them being spoken, and so Jalal's lips were forever sewn against revealing the secrets to which Shams opened his mind during those sixty days. A glimpse only was revealed to Kerra, and through her to the world.

'God save your soul,' she whispered, as the apparitions surrounded the two men. Each of them bowed before Jalal, and one laid a bouquet of flowers in front of him. Kerra clung to the jamb to prevent herself fainting. She knew her husband was far beyond her reach, but seeing the six ghostly figures, she realized she had lost him forever.

Though she knew this vision was not for her eyes, she could not break away from staring through the crack. She stood as if frozen until the *muezzin* called the evening prayer and she saw Jalal raise his head. He indicated for Shams to lead the prayer, but the older man declined.

'In the presence of such as these –', he bowed to the six figures, 'it is not proper for one so lowly as me. Jalal – *you* must lead the prayer.'

Eight figures, the corporeal ones hardly more substantial than the spirit ones, knelt to face Mecca. The beautiful voice of her husband called the prayer, and the others responded. After the prayers had finished, the figures rose as one and bowed first to Shams and then to Jalal, and then they returned from whence they came, stepping through the wall as though it were a wide open gate.

Kerra started, as though coming out of a trance, knocking the belt of her girdle against the door by accident. She saw her husband turn towards her, and she stepped away from the crack in the door. She straightened her gown and patted her hair into place as though preparing to meet an important guest. 'I have brought you some food,' she said, trying to still the flutter in her voice. She placed the brass tray on the floor, as was her custom, and was about to turn when she saw something being passed from under the door: the stem of a flower. She crouched to take the offering and gently pulled the stem until the bloom came into view. She waited, hoping that she might hear some words, but the door was firmly shut, and no sounds came from within.

Taking the flower, Kerra half-ran to her rooms, dismissing the curious looks of her servants, and shut the door behind her. She examined the unfamiliar blossom, wondering aloud what flower could bloom in the middle of winter. The petals were peach coloured and glistened as she turned them to the light, its dark green leaves shaped like an Oriental's eyes. She inhaled its perfume, and brushed the silky petals across her face, imagining them to be the fingertips of her husband. Inquisitiveness drove her to send a servant to the flower market and ask anybody if they had ever seen such a flower. The servant returned at dusk.

'None of the people of Konya have ever seen such a flower,' the servant reported. 'The flower sellers were very interested where you found it, especially in the middle of winter. I asked everywhere, ending up in the foreigners' quarters. There a spice merchant from India said he recognised the flower. It grows in his country, he said, where the sun shines hot all year round.' The servant gave the blossom back to her mistress, an enquiring look in her eyes. 'Everybody wants to know how you came by such a miracle.'

'So do I,' Kerra Hatun murmured.

Thus God revealed through the wife of Jalal of Rum some of the mysteries of the eighteen thousand worlds.

•◆•

And then after sixty days it was over. The door to the cell was thrown open, and the two men emerged into the dawn air. It was Jalal's eldest son, Sultan Walad, who saw them first. He ran to his father, but when he saw the stranger dressed in black he held back.

'Fear not,' Shams said to the youth. 'The sun is rising. Kiss his hand.'

Sultan Walad knelt to kiss his father's hand, and then Jalal spoke. 'The sun is at its zenith. Kiss his hand.' The youth hesitated and then touched his lips to the hand of Shams.

The news that Jalal had left his cell spread quickly, and a great crowd formed outside the medrese. When they saw the haggard looks of their beloved master, the people were shocked. He had gone into the cell a young man, and now look at him: his step was unsteady, his voice cracked and tuneless. But when they looked into his eyes, they saw a man aflame with life, and were humbled by what they saw.

Jalal had no will any more. He was the tool of whomever wished to use him. The townspeople wanted their imam back. They wanted lectures and discourse and guidance. And so Jalal prepared to go to the medrese, but Shams forbade it. 'I will not share sweet halwa with oxen and asses. Let them eat straw and turnip tops – Konya is full of teachers, but there is only one Jalal.' And so Jalal stayed with the other half of his heart.

From now on the two men were not to be separated. Whenever Jalal was seen walking on the street, he was always in the company of his beloved Shams, holding the older man's arm as though he was blind and being led.

When students visited his cell, many of them were perplexed. Where were the sweet words of their master? Why this silence? Why these tears when no words had been uttered, no action been taken? Some left, shaking their heads, but others recognized the silence as the voice of God, and bowed before Shams, the man who had brought Jalal to this exalted state.

Jalal's closest disciple, Husam, sought to engage Shams in mystical discourse, but when Shams was addressed he was a deaf man, rocking from side to side to a silent rhythm. When gifts or food were laid before him, he was a blind man, seeing beyond the form of things to the spinning universe of darkness and particles. When the braver students of Jalal dared to sit with the two men, they would watch as for hours Shams stared in rapt concentration of some trivial object: a feather, the hem of his gown, the sunbeam on the floor. He seemed to hear unspoken words, cry out at persons invisible to the rest of them.

Shams was a lost man, beyond the reach of normal men, a private tempest, a man of sudden rages and whirlwind moods. Though he rarely noticed people other than Jalal, the presence of some visitors to his cell was unbearable. One day a rich benefactor of the medrese visited and Shams exploded before the man had sat down. He ranted, incoherent words spat out like venom. His arms shook, as if by only the greatest force of will they were holding back from striking the startled man. Jalal bustled the merchant out of the room and hurried back to calm his distraught friend, soothing him with words and caresses like a mother with a fractious child.

Flying Shams had never spent so long in one place. He was a falcon who had found the king's wrist – what need had he for further flight? Weeks passed, and turned into months, and still the people of Konya had not heard their master's voice in the medrese. Petitions were sent to Jalal but he ignored them. Husam begged him to seek a balance in his life, but what could be found to balance one such as Shams? The sultan came to sit with the two men, but he left in silence, ashamed of his rich robes. 'These two are kings of the inner world,' he told his people. 'I have no authority here.'

Those with knowledge of such things could see the colours of Shams reflected in their master. Their noble sheikh had been taken from the sunlight of human intercourse to the dark places this stranger inhabited. Those dear eyes had seen things none of them could ever witness, and the mark of their knowledge lay across his brow. Jalal had changed: the man they saw now was deeper, broader, brighter, darker. Silence from his lips was the most beautiful music; his glance enough to cause a swoon.

And so it was that Shams of Tabriz, a dervish armed with nothing but a bamboo flute, sacked the capital of an empire.

Chapter Seven

Jalal had never known such happiness. To call this furnace that burned him day and night 'love' did no justice to its power. He had loved before: his father Baha Walad, his teacher Burhan, he loved Kerra Hatun as a man loves a wife, he loved his two sons. But this blazing emotion was new. He was entirely consumed by the other man, sleepless with joy, gripped as in a fever. He saw his friend's face in the faces of everyone he met, felt the magnificent silence of his presence in the very walls within which they sat. When his disciples begged him to speak, he could speak of nothing other than the beauty of Shams, but even then words would run dry as they failed in their task. Nothing other than Shams himself could do justice to Shams.

Try as they might, nobody understood Shams, or how to treat him. He was like a dangerous and exotic animal that would only eat from the hand of one person: Jalal.

One day Shams was alone in the street. He stood like a pillar, unmoving, staring at the ground before him. Passers-by watched him warily. What was he staring at? Was he ill? Was he mad? Hours passed, and heavy rain clouds gathered from the east. A chill was in the air, yet Shams remained unmoving. The first drops of rain scattered people indoors, yet one person remained to watch over him. Husam, because he loved his master so, loved his master's master, and worried for his safety.

The rain fell thicker, dust turning to mud.

'Please come inside, effendi,' Husam called to Shams.

The old dervish made no sign of having heard Husam. His eyes remained fixed on the ground before him. Looking closely, Husam saw the object of the man's rapt attention: a pebble, jagged and unremarkable.

Lightning flickered above the distant mountains and the rain swept across the roof tops like bolts of silk thrown out by a proud tailor. Suddenly they were in a deluge, the rutted street alive with rivulets which rushed down the hill, joining each other so that Husam found himself in a flowing gutter. The eyelids of Shams flickered as the rain gusted into his face, but still he stared without moving.

Husam stepped from under the eaves and dared to nudge the man's elbow. 'Please come inside – you are cold and wet.'

An irritable shake of the head was the only response. The man's habit was running with water, his long hair plastered over his face. The rain fell even heavier. The sky was suddenly lit by a flash of lightning, a clap of thunder almost immediately afterwards.

'Are you all right?' Husam shouted. Shams was shivering as though the lightning had entered his body. Husam hesitated and then bent to pick up the pebble. 'Please come inside.'

The dervish started, as though waking from a reverie and gave a great bellow. Husam leapt back as if struck, his arms raised before his face to protect himself, but Shams was unaware of him. He began to roar in pain, tossing his wet hair, his eyes flashing at nothing. Husam, not wanting to flee, but neither having the courage to restrain this raging man, backed away until he was pressed against the wall. The dervish stamped and cursed, his arms flailing like a man doing battle with invisible forces, the rain only tormenting him further.

A figure ran down the alley towards them, her robe over her head. She flung open the door of her house, and was about to enter when Husam called to her.

'Neighbour! Your help, please.'

'What's the trouble?' She dared not approach too close when she saw the state of Shams. 'What is he up to now?'

'Fetch Mevlana!' Husam called to the woman. 'Quickly!'

The woman ran off, leaving Husam in the company of this dancing madman. The rain began to ease, lifting as swiftly as it had descended. The inner storm of Shams was passing as well, his arms finding their place beside his body again, his curses becoming mutterings, becoming silence.

A small crowd had formed by the time Jalal came running. Shams was quiet now except for spasms which passed through him like the distant rumbling of thunder, but still the group around him kept its distance as though this was a chained bear who could not be trusted.

Husam quickly explained what had happened, and Jalal brushed the rain from his master's eyes, murmuring soft words again and again until the last eddies of the man's rage subsided.

Husam stuttered his apologies to Jalal. 'I was concerned for the health of Shams. I did not know he would act like this.'

'Your concern is to your credit.'

Jalal led Shams into his house. The crowd wanted to follow but Jalal shooed them away, allowing only Husam to enter. Shams was pacified now, and he allowed the two men to take off his wet clothes. Husam banked up the fire while Jalal tenderly dried the body of Shams and dressed him in dry robes. He then combed the old man's beard and perfumed his hair.

Husam gave the stone to Jalal. 'I did not know it was so precious.'

Chapter Seven

Jalal held the stone out to Shams, but he shook his head without looking at it. Jalal tossed it into the fireplace. 'Never disturb a man such as Shams in his reverie,' he told Husam. 'Even if you see him in danger, treat him with love and respect. Persuade him gently, but never force his eyes from the thing he desires. To break his connection in such a way is worse than plucking a baby's lips from its mother's breast and dashing its brains on a rock.'

Shams *was* a baby now, and he lay on the floor and allowed them to cover him with blankets. They waited until the eyes of the dervish had closed, and then Jalal motioned for Husam to leave. It had stopped raining so they stepped into the alley together.

The street had been transformed by the storm. The air was vibrant with energy, drops of water falling from the eaves like the dripping of diamonds. Both men sensed the change, and they paused to breathe the air deeply. The scene was flooded with yellow light from the stripe of sky between the horizon and the storm clouds, the walls of the houses seeming to dance in this strange new glow.

A messenger padded towards them, picking his way carefully through the puddles, his robe held up to his knees. He greeted Jalal respectfully and told him that the city elders had summoned him to a meeting.

Jalal and Husam followed the messenger through the muddy streets to a grand house where five of the city worthies had gathered.

Jalal bowed formally in front of them. 'How can I assist you?'

'What is this on your head?' one of the men asked irritably.

Jalal had replaced his professor's turban with a simple felt hat, the *kulah* of a dervish. The conical hat was the form of the tombstone, signifying that the wearer was one who had died before death. 'Jalal is no longer here,' he said simply. 'Look for him in the graveyard.'

'See?' the man said, turning to his neighbour. '*This* is what I mean! What sort of answer is that?'

A mild faced man, who had studied with Jalal's father, held his hands up as though he was pacifying a fractious horse. 'Calm yourself. I am certain he will see sense.' He turned to Jalal. 'Once again, this Shams of Tabriz has caused a disturbance. How long will this continue?'

'For as long as God wills.'

'Or Satan,' the first man said. 'We are not convinced who this *malamati* takes his orders from.'

'If you opened the window of your heart you would see clearly enough,' he said softly.

The council leader raised his hands again. 'We will not argue about this matter. We brought you here not to talk about Shams, but to make a request.' The five men turned their eyes on Jalal. 'We want you to open the medrese.'

Jalal shrugged. 'What can I say to my students? There are no words left.'

'Has everything changed so much?'

'An accident of the heart has befallen me,' Jalal said. 'I can do nothing other than tremble in the presence of God.'

'But you have responsibilities.'

'My first duty is to God.'

'And your second duty?'

'Is to Shams.'

A clicking of tongues and shaking of heads conveyed the disapproval of the group. 'Your declarations of love are too much,' an elderly sheikh counselled. 'People are calling it blasphemy.'

'I worship him,' Jalal said with a sudden laugh. 'He is everything to me.'

'Beware, my dear Jalal,' another man said. 'The town is unhappy with this stranger. They will tolerate him only as long as you remain their master. Don't give away your professor's robes, or you will no longer be their master.'

'I never was their master.'

'You are turning from the faith,' the first man said testily. '*That* is what we mean.'

'Friend,' Jalal said, grasping the man's hand. 'This *is* the faith. The way of God is the way of love.'

The man uncurled Jalal's fingers from his wrist and tossed it away. '*La ilaha il al-Llah,*' he said as if it was a curse. 'There is no God, but God.'

'Yes,' Jalal said. 'And God does not live in the medrese or the mosque or even in the *Kaabe*. He lives here –' He laid his hand on the chest of the man, and gazed at him with love, 'in our hearts.'

•◆•

'What did they want?' Shams asked when Jalal returned. The dervish had changed back into his patched robes even though they were still damp.

'They want me to open the medrese.'

'And will you?'

'I will do what you tell me.'

'Then we will get drunk together, you and me,' Shams announced.

Jalal knew he was being tested, but still he hesitated. For an imam to drink liquor would bring disgrace and public condemnation far greater than had already been expressed.

There was nothing for Jalal to say: it was no use protesting against the request, explaining the censure that such an act would bring. It was pointless questioning the intent of Shams, for the master has only one purpose for his student: liberation from all that holds him back from full submission to God. Submission to the teacher is the first step on that path. But although Jalal trusted Shams, he had been trained well in matters of morality. The commandment forbidding the drinking of wine was no minor prohibition, and Jalal had never allowed strong liquor to touch his lips. He had made his home in the nest of the Shari'ah, the religious law; but if a fledgling is to fly, it needs to leave the nest as surely as it left the egg, and abandon itself to the mystery of flight. If Shams wanted him to drink wine, he would do so, even if it meant falling to his destruction.

The *muezzin* began to call the early evening prayer and Jalal got to his feet. 'I will send a servant to the Hebrews' ward,' he said quietly.

'*You* will fetch it and bring it to me at the medrese.'

'It is *maghrib*. May I perform my prayers first?'

'I want it *now*.'

And so he fell from the nest. Jalal walked to the wine sellers' quarter as though in a dream. He watched himself buying a flask of wine, paying for it, carrying it through the streets. The news quickly spread, and a crowd followed him back to the college. He was aware of the whispers and the pointing fingers, and his soul was stung as though by the flails of a whip. Though he had never sought approval, it had always been his: he was Jalal, the son of Baha Walad, an ascendant star in the blessed sky above Konya. He had been one of them, and yet not one of them: he had been better, more pious, uncontaminated by sin. Now he was becoming infected by the man they called Shamsi Perende – Flying Shams.

Jalal's cheeks burned. He wanted to protest, explain himself to the crowd, but what could he say? That he would follow Shams to the end of the earth, even to hell if he was asked? He murmured prayers, stepping carefully lest he spill any of the forbidden liquid.

Worshippers were leaving the mosque as he passed, and their eyes were drawn to the crowd. 'What is happening?' they called.

'See what has befallen our master,' a voice called back. 'Buying wine in public, getting drunk with that vagabond.'

'Shame on you!' another voice cried. 'May Allah punish your transgression.'

It was like a weight falling from his shoulders. Suddenly Jalal gave up the need to defend himself. He opened his heart to their denunciation, allowing the acid of their remarks to burn away layer upon layer of his self-importance. As he did so, something else took the place of humiliation. He smiled to himself, though he did not know why. His limbs were light and his senses sharp. The cool breeze that blew from the mountains passed straight through him; there was no obstruction, just a vast, glorious space where his pain had been.

Jalal was nowhere to be seen by the time the crowd reached the medrese: he had ceased to exist. The man they called by that name held the flask to Shams, not a single drop spilt, but the Jalal of Jalal was not there. He was everywhere.

'Sun of Tabriz, I am your slave, your servant, your wine bearer,' he said. 'If you order me to drink this wine, I will. If you order me to drink poison, I will.'

Shams took the wine flask and addressed the crowd. This was the first time many had heard his voice, and they craned to hear his words. 'I have tested your master. Nowhere have I met such devotion. Truly is the lowest highest, the highest lowest. Truly this slave is a king, this servant a master, this wine bearer the source of the wine.'

Saying this, he poured the wine onto the ground and bowed to Jalal.

Such public displays only added to the ill feeling many of the town felt towards Shams. How could the people of Konya understand Shams, and the transformation that had been wrought in their master? They saw the man lost to the world, and called him mad. They saw the outward signs of intoxication, and blamed wine. They saw the embraces, the kisses, the adoration, and believed it was lust they witnessed. They saw one man worshipping another, and cried 'sacrilege'.

Jalal's disciples came to him and begged him to give up this infatuation. The man is a tramp, they said. Arrogant and uneducated. Where is his authority? Where his marks of office? Who has he studied with to be so much the master of you? If he is such a master, where are the signs of illumination? He looks no different from a poor peasant.

'The outward show of a sheikh is not important,' Jalal said. 'The only need for a teacher is that he possesses all that a disciple needs.' Jalal searched their faces for signs of understanding, but all he saw was the frowns of their concern. How could they not see the brilliance of the Sun? Why did they feel threatened by one who meant them no harm?

Jalal then told his disciples a story: There was once an inquisitive lion cub who wandered away from the pride to explore his surroundings. After many adventures, the cub became lost. Searching in vain for his family, he came across a flock of sheep who adopted him. In time, the cub forgot he was a lion and came to identify himself with the sheep. He ate grass like a sheep, made the sound of a sheep, acted and thought like a sheep. One day, when the cub had grown up, another lion passed by – he was very old and scarred, and was finding a place to spend his last days. The flock was terrified and it scattered, including the adopted lion. The old lion, seeing the curious sight of one of his kind living among sheep, crept closer and closer to the startled flock. 'Hey,' he called. 'What are you doing? Don't you realise you're a lion?' 'You're mistaken,' the young lion called back. 'I am a sheep. I live like a sheep, and sound like a sheep. Listen.' He gave a cry which *did* sound like a sheep. The older lion took him to a pond. 'Look in the water. Does that look like a sheep?' The lion had to admit it didn't – in fact, it looked like a lion. 'I will teach you to be a lion again,' the old male said. So, day by day the older lion gave him lessons in how to roar. Though the lessons were difficult, and though many times the student despaired, he discovered that day by day he sounded less like a sheep. Finally, the day came when he gave his first roar. 'I *am* a lion!' he exclaimed, turning to his friend. But the old lion had slunk off on his journey, continuing to look for a place to spend the last of his days.

'Shams is the lion, we are the lost cubs,' Jalal said.

'*You* are the young lion,' one of the disciples said. 'The rest of us are sheep, and we have much to fear from a lion.'

'Even if we eat nothing but grass all our lives, we are all lions – every one of us. We have nothing to fear from Shams.'

Nothing more was said to Jalal, but gossip spread among the people of Konya. They were not convinced by the few disciples who sought to defend their master. 'When Shams appears in public, he looks either drunk or mad, a no-good *qalandar* who had bewitched our beloved imam.'

The barrel was unstaunched, and criticism flowed like bad vinegar. 'He is barely civilized,' they complained. 'The rare times he visits the mosque, he weeps so loudly that prayers are interrupted.'

'We have tried to love him because we love our Mevlana, but he spurns our approaches, dismissive of even the most esteemed authority.'

Husam dared to beg Shams to show respect to others, but the older man refused. 'There is the law of man and the law of God,' he said. 'I will follow only one master.'

With each day, enmity against Shams grew, and rumours about him spread. Kerra Hatun had fallen ill – he had placed a curse on her. The man was a fakir, in league with Satan. People had seen him through the window of the cell performing a whirling dance, heard strange cries of ecstasy that chilled the bone.

The more that people sought to pull Jalal away from Shams, the tighter the grip of the old dervish became. His jealousy grew and he forbade any more visitors, furious at anyone who dared interrupt their reveries. Again, the doors of the cell were closed, and only Husam and the youth Sultan Walad were allowed entrance.

Sometimes Jalal wished that it was over, that he could return to Kerra and his children, that he could rest on the padded professor's chair, let his mind slide into indolence, indulge his senses. When his resolve wavered Shams would slap his face, shake him violently, shout abuse so that those who listened at the door feared for Jalal's safety.

Such lack of compromise has a cost. Now when Shams was met on the street alone, he was assailed with insults. Swords were drawn against him, fists clenched, dogs set on him until it was dangerous for him to step outside.

Shams took his complaints to Jalal. 'These people treat me like an enemy. Yesterday a man spat at me.' He wiped his face and showed his hand to Jalal as though the spittle was still there. 'Is this town so stupid they cannot see a friend when one is in their midst?'

'Take no notice of them – they mean no harm.'

'They mean a great *deal* of harm! They will drive me away from you.'

'You are the light of my house. Do not go away and leave me alone.' Jalal seized his friend's hand and kissed it fervently.

'They are *your* followers – cannot you control them?'

'I tell them to respect you. I say that if they love me, then they must love you, but they have minds of their own.'

Shams could not stay in this town, and he could not ask Jalal to leave. It had been the pure presence of Jalal that had calmed the restlessness of Shams; now that their seclusion was disturbed, his agitation returned. If Konya would not allow Shams to love his friend, then Shams could not remain.

None saw the dervish in his black felt robes enter Konya, and none saw him leave. The beloved friend of Jalal had flown.

Chapter Eight

The empty cell where Shams had stayed took on new dimensions now the dervish had gone: to Jalal's eyes the room was huge, as though it had once been filled with tables and chairs and now that its owner had gone, all other objects had been taken with him. Such emptiness where there had been such fullness.

Jalal sent out students to search the mosques and alleys of Konya, but no sign of their quarry was reported. Again and again Jalal returned to the cell, but it was as empty as ever. The whitewashed stone wall was deaf to his questioning, the floor insolent in its silence.

'Where is he?' Jalal broke the string which bound the mattress and searched through the straw. He turned the sleeping pallet over and searched the ground underneath as though Shams could be hiding there.

He ran to his own quarters. 'Where have you hidden him?' he demanded of Kerra. 'You have taken him against his will.' He pulled open the cabinet in which she kept their clothes, he searched the privy, the storeroom, he pulled pans and bowls from their places heedless of what was broken.

'Tell me what have you done with him,' he ordered the crowd which gathered outside to stare. 'You hate him and want him gone. Where is he?' he seized an old man and stared into his eyes. 'Murdered?'

Jalal turned, not waiting for a reply, and Husam ran after him. 'Master, control your passion. If Shams has gone, it was his will which caused it.'

'You cannot know what pain our separation is causing him,' Jalal snapped at his old friend. 'Bring him back to me.'

'If I could bring him back, I would, but Shams has disappeared.'

Jalal shut himself in his cell, ignoring the soothing infusion of herbs that Kerra brought. When his disciples came to calm their master, he refused to speak; when they pressed him, he cursed them. These were the people who had driven the sun from the sky by their small-minded jealousy.

'He has lost all control,' people said.

'Shams has cast a spell over him.'

And so he had – the spell of love. No black magic here, this was not the work of an ambitious mind, nothing twisted. This was the heart of Jalal unfolding like a rose, Shams the gardener watering the flower with care and attention.

And yet, as each petal unfurled, so another layer of his soul was exposed like raw skin. The door of his cell remained locked as he howled his grief and anger. None were there to see him tear his clothes, strike his head with his hands till blood ran. Kerra knelt outside the door, weeping at what she heard, refusing the ministrations of her neighbours. She heard him cursing Shams for making him love him. She pressed her forehead to the floor as he cursed God, praying that he be forgiven.

Kerra bore his pain for three days and then she brought two strong men to the door and had them break it down. Jalal was curled in the corner like a whipped dog. The men carried him outside where they washed him, combed his beard, and took away the rags that he wore. When they brought his professor's robes, he refused to wear them, insisting instead on the patched robes of a dervish.

Those who had criticised Shams, seeing their master so stricken, repented their words and acts. Some came to him to beg his forgiveness. The storm had gone now, and he gave it freely. 'I was ill,' he said simply, his voice hoarse. 'I was under the power of a fakir. I am purified now.'

Jalal had been washed clean by his tears, but it was as though his soul too had been washed away in the torrent.

He was placid in a way Kerra had never seen, succumbing to her will as he had never done before. She fed him goat's broth and barley bread, massaged the life back into his hands and feet, oiled his hair, coaxing her dear husband back into life. Not once did she make mention of Shams – the scorching sun who had flown into their lives and flown out just as suddenly.

Jalal had the fragile air of a man made of glass, as if any sudden movement or loud noise would shatter him. He spoke little, and then with his voice lowered. His movements were cautious, his emotions muted.

He was beyond consolation. At dawn the watchman would find him lost, stray dogs at his heels, and he would lead his imam home, his heart breaking to see such a one as this brought so low. Husam took Jalal to the infirmary at Divigri, where he sat beside the beautiful watercourse designed to soothe those troubled in spirit, but the groaning of the waterwheel sounded like the groans of torture. 'This cry is my voice,' he said. 'This flowing water, my tears.'

When the elders came to him with his professor's robes, they did not disguise their pleasure at the absence of Shams. There would be a brief period of mourning perhaps, they reasoned, but soon he will be ours again. And sure enough, he let them dress him. When they asked him to return to his chair in the medrese, he did not resist. His disciples celebrated. 'At last we are to have our master back.'

'The greatest Konya has ever known.'

'Greater than Ibn Arabi, greater than Attar!'

The medrese was crowded on the morning of Jalal's first sermon. Sheikhs and emirs from far and wide came to Konya to witness the return of this illustrious imam. The whole of Konya was restless with anticipation. Gossip was rife.

'I have heard that our Mevlana had condemned Shams.'

'And so he should – the man was a charlatan.'

Sultan Walad led his father through the crowd to the speaker's chair. The murmur of voices stilled as they watched their imam. Jalal rested his hand on his son's shoulder as a blind man would, looking neither to the left nor the right. He lowered himself into his chair, exhausted, and everyone in the audience turned to his neighbour.

'Is he ill?'

'See how he has aged. Look at his grey hairs.'

'He looks too weak to speak.'

Jalal pushed himself to his feet. The effort seemed to pain him, and those at the back of the room craned to see if the master was about to fall.

Jalal lifted his hands, and silence fell. 'You want me to speak.'

'We have missed you,' a voice called out.

'And what do you wish me to speak of?' He searched the faces of those who sat before him. His eyes were so piercing that many could not face him, and they dropped their gaze to the floor. Nobody spoke.

'I will talk of Shams, then.'

Jalal did not notice the restless movement in the crowd, nor hear the muttering of disapproval.

'If I did not see his face in all of your faces, I could not stand here,' Jalal began. 'If I was truly cut from the source of my life, I would be like a foetus torn from the womb. How then could I survive?'

The voices of dissent were louder, but Jalal was deaf to the effect of his words.

'Shams is the ground on which I walk. He is the air I breathe. His eyes are the eyes of all that look at me, his lips every mouth that utters every word.'

He was crying now, no longer addressing the audience, lost in his grief. 'I bid my eyes to not weep, but they disobey me. How should I not weep when the sun falls from the sky? I command my hands not to pluck the air, but they defy me.'

'Fulfil your duty!' a voice cried from the back. 'Speak to us of religious matters, not this man.'

Jalal noticed the crowd for the first time, and placed his fingers over his mouth as though to staunch the words, but it was too late. Sultan Walad looked at his father, and he saw him as the others must have: distracted, his eyes darting from left to right – a madman. Jalal was staring at something at the back of the room, his address forgotten. Sultan Walad turned to see the object of his scrutiny, but saw nothing unusual.

'What are you looking at?' he whispered as his father continued to stare.

'That figure in white who is standing at the back of the hall. Who is it?' He shaded his eyes with a hand. 'Who are you, effendi?' he called.

Heads turned to see whom he was addressing.

'Yes, *you*.' His shaking finger pointed at the figure.

'There is nobody there, father,' Sultan Walad murmured, taking his father's arm and forcing it down.

A sheikh from the distant town of Sivas rose, and his followers behind him. 'This is madness,' he declared. 'The rose of Rum has turned rotten.' He swept from the room, followed by his murids. Others left, some hesitated at the door. The majority stayed seated, one or two weeping to see their imam so lost.

Husam took Jalal by the arm and tried to lead him from the platform, but he resisted, his eyes still fixed on the figure that only he could see. 'Help me here,' Husam hissed at Sultan Walad.

His son took Jalal's other arm and they guided him off the platform. Jalal's head twisted behind him to keep his eyes on the stranger in white. 'Elias!' he said suddenly. 'It is Elias!'

'Hush, Mevlana,' Husam said. 'Do not provoke these people.'

'I see him! I see the prophet Elias!'

The faces of all men were present in those of the crowd as they led Jalal away: compassion, anger, fear, resentment, condemnation, disgust. Love.

Kerra Hatun hurried to take her husband from Sultan Walad, ignoring the cruel comments from behind her. Thus held between the two who loved him most, Jalal was led from the medrese, away from the dome which his father had made shine with his glorious reputation, only for his son to tarnish.

•◆•

It was that night he heard the sounds of the *rebap* and *ney* from the open window of a house. Clapping and singing too.

Jalal stood by the window as if spellbound. His heart raced as he listened to the weaving of flute and strings and voices. 'Beloved!' he cried. He hammered on the door, but nobody heard, so he pushed it open.

A wedding party was in progress. Jalal snatched a lantern from the wall and examined each face, searching for the grey beard and black eyes of Shams. The host did not recognise the imam. He thought a stranger was here to cause trouble, and he wrestled him to the door until someone called out for him to stop.

'Effendi!' the host cried, recognizing him now. 'Are you drunk?'

'I must be.'

The host leant close to Jalal to smell his breath. Jalal seized the man's head and whispered fiercely in his ear. 'I am drunk with love.'

The man pulled away, embarrassed. 'Effendi, please eat with us.'

'I am full – what need have I for food?'

The room was silent, the festivities suspended.

'Musicians, play on so I may hear my Beloved in your voices,' Jalal called.

The musicians hesitated. They barely recognized this haggard face before them. Gone were the professor's robes and turban, the regal bearing, the air of quiet. Here stood a stranger in the patched robes and hat of a dervish, his eyes blazing, his hands trembling. And now he was calling for music – this from an imam who had always forbidden it in his presence. Jalal took all the coins from his pockets and showered the musicians with gold and silver. 'Play on, or else I may wake up again.'

The host nodded to the players and so they played, reluctantly at first, but as the spark of music caught, so the fire was lit. The festivities began again and as the music rose, so did the arms of Jalal. Slowly at first, and then faster, he turned on the spot, the skirts of his robe swirling out. His arms were outstretched now, his right palm up, receiving the grace of God, the left palm down, transmitting it to the earth. Those who watched noticed his lips moving as he silently repeated the name of God. His head was tilted to one side, his eyes downcast as he spun faster and faster. The musicians caught his passion and increased the tempo, the *kudum* player drumming in time with the slap of Jalal's feet on the stone floor.

The other dancers had paused to watch him. Surely he would fall over, lose his balance and crash into the walls? But no – with perfect poise, Jalal whirled, just as Shams had taught him. This was the *sema*, the dervish mystical dance whose origins were hidden.

With each revolution Jalal was erased, and in his place was manifesting something else, something that was not something. The centre of his body, around which he turned was now the centre of the world. Everything in existence: this room and all the people in it, Konya and all its inhabitants, the land of Anatolia, the countries beyond that and the far continents where people lived lives unaware of this stuffy room – all revolved around the spinning figure in its centre. Everything in the world: deserts and mountains, forests and jungles and every creature at the bottom of every ocean were the flax spun from this wheel. And beyond that, at the furthest reaches of God's imagination were the sun and the moon and the stars, the seen and the unseen worlds, and all these revolved around this single point. And at the centre of this point was nothing but stillness and absence. No *thing* existed anymore, just *being*.

As the figure of their imam continued to turn, so words began to come, tumbling one after the other.

What have you done to me?
I was an ascetic, independent of the world
Now my feet are lifted against my will
this body turns in spite of itself.
And if I stop my ears with my fingers
The music plays only louder.
I tried to hide my heart
but you found it and stole it
and now nothing of myself remains
but this puppet which turns and turns.

Some of the wedding guests were shocked by what they heard. 'Now he has become nothing but a *kahin*,' they said indignantly, 'Just the type of drunken shaman the Prophet Muhammad warned us against.'

'Will you continue to allow this performance?' they complained to the host. But the host was deaf to their complaints. Yes, this was unorthodox, probably not according to *sunnah*. Yes, it was not what they expected from the son of Baha Walad. But the man's heart responded to that of this turning figure. Propriety had no place here.

'Allah! ' Jalal cried aloud, a shout echoed by others. 'Allah! Allah!'

Some of the guests left, but those who remained began to lose themselves, too – not with the drunkenness of wine, but with a far more refined liquor. Some of them began to follow the movements of Jalal, their feet obeying not the command of their owners, but that of a higher source. And as they whirled, their arms also raised to heaven, and they too gave themselves to God.

The music continued till dawn. When one musician tired, another took his place. As the string of the *oud* snapped, so the *rebab* took over. And as they played, so Jalal never ceased to whirl and the words continued to come unbidden to his lips.

I came with an empty cup
and asked you to fill it.
You knocked the cup from my hand
and as I bent to gather the pieces
you gave me the vineyard.
I asked for water
you gave me wine.
I asked for bread
you gave me this table.
I asked for salvation
you destroyed me.

Kerra wandered the city that night, her concern for Jalal mounting with every empty street she searched. At each of the twelve city gates she asked the watchmen if they had seen the imam, but none had. At last she found him on the walls of the citadel, gazing out over the moat into the darkness, searching the gloom for something.

'What are you looking for, husband?'

He addressed his answer to the horizon, though the word was but a murmur. 'Shams,' he said.

'Come home, husband.'

He turned to her, puzzled, and she took his hand and led him through the awakening streets of the town. Jalal realized how exhausted he was. He would have lain in the street and slept there and then, but Kerra chivvied him, half carrying him the final distance. Brief convulsions of words still spilled from his lips, though now they were half formed, an echo of the earlier songs.

Jalal seemed to come to his senses when he was lying on his sleeping pallet. 'What is happening to me?' he asked his wife, as she watched over him with such concern. 'Whose words were those?'

'Hush now.'

His eyelids flickered. He was on the very edge of sleep. 'Cover me,' he said. His voice was that of a child.

She brought a second cloak and draped it over him. In the early morning light his face was ashen, his cheeks sunken.

'Am I possessed, like they say, by a *djinn*?'

'Shh.'

He seemed to sleep, but his lips moved so she leant over him. 'This is the first peace I have felt since he left,' Jalal whispered. 'You are a good woman.'

Watching the beloved face of her husband as he slept, Kerra saw such sweet joy that she wept in spite of her own pain. There was no madness here, this was no possession. She had seen the same look on the face of women as they slept after childbirth. Jalal was being born to himself, and in the act of delivery was the death of the old. The cries and groans and ecstatic dances were both birth pangs and death throes.

'Send me the strength, O God, to be the wife of this man,' she whispered. 'And if it be thy will, return Shams to him.'

Chapter Nine

Kerra turned to Jalal's friend. 'Husam, why can he not let the man go?' she said. 'This attachment is destroying him.'

Husam sighed. Jalal and Kerra were like a brother and sister to him. His heart was pained twice over to see them undergo such suffering. But he was a wise man, and he knew that Jalal was in the grip of something far greater than Shams.

He thought for a moment, and then told Kerra a story he had heard from the lips of his friend: 'There was once a schoolteacher who lived in the mountains,' Husam began. 'He was so poor that he had just a single cotton robe to wear. One winter's day, when the river was swollen with flood, a bear was washed along in the current, tumbling head over heels. The students seeing the flash of fur called out. 'Teacher, teacher! A fur coat has fallen into the water. Quick! Pull it out.' The desperate teacher jumped into the river to catch the coat, but the bear, seeing a chance to save its own life, suddenly plunged its claws into him and hung on for dear life. 'Teacher!' the children cried, seeing their teacher thrashing and being pulled under. 'Come back to the river bank – it's not worth drowning for the sake of a coat.' The teacher, his mouth full of water, called back, 'I'm *trying* to let go! It's the fur coat – it won't let go of me!'

Kerra smiled wanly. Shams *was* like a wild bear, but still the parable was false. Her husband, she wanted to tell Husam, was *not* freezing on a river bank. Not only had he winter clothes, but he lived in a house warm with love. Why throw himself into this river to grapple with Shams? He should have stayed on the river bank with the rest of the townspeople, thrown rocks and fired arrows if this bear had tried to climb out.

But for all her enmity towards Shams, if Kerra Hatun had known his whereabouts, she would have brought Shams back to Konya. She had seen her husband undergo many trials of suffering on the path, but none approached this. He had endured mortifications of the body without a murmur, he had fought his lower self and never cried out. But the loss of Shams was agony. She tried to understand his feelings, why the absence of a man who six months ago was a stranger should seem such a death to him, but they were foreign to her. She asked Jalal to explain himself, but he was beyond reasoning. When he opened his mouth to speak, poems flew out. When he gestured with his hands, they began to dance. When he tried to tell her with his eyes, they cried too much.

Jalal had become a great lover of music. For hours, through the day and the night, musicians played for him, half glad and half in awe of the desperate joy they inspired. Music was not an escape for Jalal, neither too were the poems which continued to flood from him; rather, they were the plunging into the river whose banks Kerra dared not leave. Had Jalal been more the master of his passion, he might have likewise resisted the flood, but try as he may, the bank upon which he stood gave no foothold. Where other people found solid ground, he found slippery mud. And where other people found icy water, he found release. Yes, he was drowning in the grip of a wild bear, but he welcomed his death.

News had quickly spread of Jalal's dancing, and spontaneous songs. An imam dancing in public with wine drinkers and women? And this sudden mania for music? Those who did not condemn him, pitied him, thinking that he had lost his senses.

The months of silence with Shams collapsed into verse, and they spilled from him, too quick to write. Too many words, none of them good enough, not one of them with the power to bring Shams back.

Guards, go to your watch tower.
Bring news of every stranger to me –
Shamsi Tabriz could be passing your way.
Let no man call himself a Muslim
who fails to report sight of the sun to me.

The poems were passed from hand to hand around the town. Jalal had signed them 'Hamush' – the silent one – but everybody knew the hand from whence they came, and they all marvelled at the change wrought in their author.

•◆•

Nearly half a year passed before the first report of Shams was received. A trader was brought before Jalal.

'Tell my father what you told me,' Sultan Walad said.

Bewildered at the excitement caused by his news, the young Syrian stammered. 'Shams of Tabriz has been seen.'

The bowed figure in front of him lifted its head from its chest. Jalal had aged: his cheeks were lined and more grey hairs clustered round at his temples. The young trader flinched at the eyes that blazed from their sunken sockets.

'The one they call the Flier,' he added when Jalal said nothing.

'Where?' Jalal croaked at last.

'In Damascus, effendi.'

'When?'

'Two moons ago.'

'Thanks be to God, the eclipse of my sun has ended.' He forced himself to his feet and began to struggle out of his robe.

'What are you doing, father?' Sultan Walad asked in alarm.

'I have nothing left to give this messenger but my shirt.'

Husam took his master's arm and made him sit while Sultan Walad gave the Syrian a silver coin before ushering him from the room.

'Husam, bring me paper. I will write a letter to my Beloved.'

His hand trembled as he penned the words:

Return to your home, O friend of mine –
a place has been made ready in my heart.
Pillows and fine carpets cover the marble floor
and incense burns in its holder.
Your chair is ready; no one has sat there
lest the shape you left behind be erased.
No one has drunk from goblets
nor eaten from plates since your going away.
Everything is as you left it –
even the dust is undisturbed.

The letter was sent by the swiftest camel, the driver well paid not to dally. Barely had the man left, and Jalal was watching from the city wall.

O that the desert was a map,
to be so easily folded,
Rum the neighbour of Damascus.
O that time could pass
as in sleep,
Ninety days, my tomorrow.

Now that there was a target for the arrows of Jalal's poetry, he fired hundreds of letters, showering them onto the town of Damascus. With such an onslaught, Jalal told himself, *one* must find its goal – the heart of Shams.

A month passed and there was no reply. Two months passed and there was still no reply.

Shams, my soul, have mercy on me
I have been crushed by the feet of your absence.
Have mercy on me,
for I am destroyed in your name.

He paid children to watch the roads into Konya, to call him as soon as they saw a messenger from Shams. But no messenger came. Sometimes travellers came with spurious sightings of Shams. He was in Tabriz, in Aleppo, in Tarsus.

Husam tried to protect his master from these jackals, but Jalal would entertain all of them, no matter how thinly disguised their lying. One day, Husam could stand it no longer.

'Do you not know you are being taken advantage of? These people are telling you lies, just to get your money.'

'If I thought they were telling the truth,' Jalal told him, 'I would not give them money – I would give them my life.'

And then it happened. A message from Shams. He was in Damascus, awaiting reunion with his master and servant, Jalal. *Alhamdulillah* – all praise belongs to God!

Jalal wanted to go, but his sons begged him not to: it was a long journey, dangerous for one so weakened by grief.

'I will go with my brother,' Alaeddin said. 'We will bring him back - by force if needed.'

Jalal waved his younger son away. 'Shams must be coaxed back with promises of love and many fine gifts. You will stay behind. Sultan Walad will go.'

He did not see the scowl of Alaeddin, nor did he hear the argument between the two brothers when they left the room. 'Why should you be the one to go? Why are you always favoured?'

'I am older than you – and wiser.'

'What use will your books be if you meet robbers?' Alaeddin sneered. 'What will you do to attackers – preach them to death?'

'I have been chosen – you have not,' Sultan Walad said with a shrug, so like Jalal. 'Will you defy our father?'

Of course he would not. And so Sultan Walad set off for Damascus with a caravan of twenty men and left his brother to his rage. Sultan Walad took two purses of silver coins donated by Mu'inuddin, the chief minister, rich carpets and brassware, presents to tempt the sun of Tabriz to return with them. They slept in their saddles for two nights out of three, pausing only to water the mules. Through sunbaked landscapes they hurried, over the treacherous Taurus mountains, passing caravanserais in the night.

'What is your hurry, stranger?' others called to them.

What could they say? We are bringing the sun back to Konya before our master goes blind for want of light?

They found Shams playing chess with a Frankish monk in the courtyard of an inn. He looked up at Sultan Walad, and allowed his hand to be kissed. Shams took the letter that Sultan Walad had brought from his father, but left it unread on the table.

'The people of Konya beg your forgiveness,' Sultan Walad said, repeating the message of the letter. 'They, like my father, await your return with impatience.'

Shams nodded, but said nothing. Sultan Walad, worried that his journey was in vain, and that he would have to return to Konya alone, laid all the gifts on the ground before Shams.

The dervish shrugged. 'What need have I for these trinkets? Give them to the poor of this district so that they may buy food. In the company of Jalal, I no longer need food.'

'You will return to Konya?'

'I cannot disobey.'

This was a new Shams: no longer sparking with rage and impatience, he seemed to be cloaked in silence, as though all sound was being absorbed by his body.

Sultan Walad murmured his thanks to God. 'Then we must hurry back.'

'There are three requirements of the spiritual path,' Shams said sternly. 'The first is a tongue which repeats the name of God. The second is a heart which offers thanks to God. The third is a body which waits patiently.'

Sultan Walad began to thank the sheikh for the gift of his wisdom, but Shams brushed the youth aside. 'You will rest. I will finish my game.' With that, he returned to his chess game with the Frankish monk.

It was two days later when they set off. Though there were mules to spare, Sultan Walad refused to ride, instead walking beside Shams' horse and leading it himself. When the old dervish protested, the youth begged that he not be forced into an act of disrespect. 'You are my master's master, and therefore I am doubly your slave. It is not proper for me to ride in your presence.'

Shams was so pleased with the son of his friend that he shared many secrets with him on the journey. While the older man rode and the disciple held the bridle, Shams spoke of the Qur'an and the way of the dervish, and when he ceased speaking he taught him through his heart. Veils were torn from the eyes of Sultan Walad, revealing the wonders of the inner landscape they passed through. At night when their bodies rested, Sultan Walad passed through the other worlds, returning to tell Shams of his dreams in the morning.

He tried to remember the three requirements: silently repeating the holy name, thanking God for bad as well as good, and slowing his pace to that of Shams, but the night before they reached Konya, Sultan Walad's youthful impatience got the better of him and he sent ahead a rider on a fleet-footed camel to deliver the news to his father. The long night was over – the sun of Tabriz was returning to Konya.

Even before the *muezzin* called the sleeping town to prayer the next morning, the silhouette of a man could be seen standing alone on the city walls. On his head was the tomb-shaped hat of a dervish, and looking closely, an observer would have seen his robe was patched and threadbare.

The figure was motionless, gazing to the mountains of the east, towards the rising sun and Damascus, just as he had gazed on a similar spring morning almost a year before, when Shams had yet to enter his life.

This was the time of day that Jalal loved the most. He breathed the cool air, tasting the scent of wood smoke on the breeze, and for the first time in months, he realized he was hungry. A street vendor pushed his barrow through the arch beneath his feet, cursing as the wheels jammed in a rut. A passer-by was called over and together they shoved the barrow, unaware they were being watched from above. Jalal realized how much he loved the people of this city, their passion, their ignorance, their wisdom, their humanity.

The long night had come to an end, the sun claiming back the heavens from the stars. Today was the day that Shams was coming home.

As the morning progressed, more and more people heard the news and joined Jalal on the city walls. When the sun was at its zenith there were two hundred people present – scholars and merchants, artisans and peasants, Muslims and Christians and Jews, all waiting for sight of the caravan. Some were there to welcome Shams, some to cast disapproving looks: the news of the dervishs' return was received in many ways.

It was a child who saw the dust in the distance. 'Look!' His elders strained their eyes to see, but then dismissed it as nothing. Then another person raised an arm to point. 'It's them!'

And so it was – twenty men, mules and camels, riding at full speed. At the front was the horse of Shams, its rider laughing with strong white teeth, a youth running beside him.

Jalal was the fruit in the hand of the city, held out in front while the crowd stood back. Shams reined his horse to a halt in front of Jalal, dust and pebbles flying in the air. Sparks seemed to flicker from the man's eyes as he was helped down to the ground. The two men embraced and then Jalal fell to the feet of his beloved, while a *hafiz* recited the Qur'an beside them.

First He kills me
and then He takes me in his arms.

The crowd surged forward to witness the meeting of the two great oceans, and for a moment they could not tell Jalal from Shams, Shams from Jalal.

Chapter Ten

Those who truly loved Jalal welcomed the return of Shams as they might welcome death into a house of suffering. They knew they may lose their master, that his beloved face may never be seen again, but their compassion for Jalal compelled them to accept this dangerous stranger. If the presence of the dervish delivered their beloved Mevlana from his agony, then they would open the door and greet him. The mystic dance of the *sema* was performed all day and late into the night, the chanting of devotional songs pouring from the open windows of the medrese. Some of those who had insulted and vilified Shams, seeing the fruit of their deeds in their master's suffering, now came to apologize, bringing gifts which he accepted and distributed to the poor. There was no lacking of false smiles, however, no shortage of hands held out in friendship which concealed hidden knives. Jalal, blind with joy, saw no such things, but Shams, for all his sideways glances and seeming ignorance saw the heart behind every action.

Jalal was complete. He sat between Shams and Kerra, his two sons at his feet. It was a feast without food, a wedding where every guest was both bride and groom. Poems flooded the room until one by one the guests slipped away into the night, their bodies and clothes soaked in the intoxicating liquor of the celebration, and Jalal slept.

He woke as the first smudge of light entered the sky. Still drunk with happiness from the night before, he nevertheless recognized a speck of discontent in his joy. There was a question which he could not brush aside. He lit a candle and went to the room of Shams where he found his friend kneeling, his back to the door, swaying as he repeated the name of God. Without opening his eyes, or breaking the rhythm of his movement, Shams spoke. 'You have a question.'

There was silence as the rocking continued. Jalal felt a dribble of wax run over his fingers. 'Why did you leave Konya?' he said at last.

'I was driven away.'

'But why did you *stay* away?' *That* was the question Jalal needed answering.

'I never left you,' Shams said, his back still to Jalal. 'How could I abandon you? We two are one.'

'But why no word from you? You were so cruel.'

'My silence was my lesson for you, my absence a test.'

The *muezzin* called the *azan*. The call to prayer was the most beautiful of the dawn birdsong, and Jalal waited for its completion before he asked his next question.

'Did I pass?'

'Yes...and no.'

Shams explained. Jalal had been a heifer tied between two masters: the elders of Konya, and Shams himself. A beast with two masters is owned by neither, and yet is doubly a chattel, so Shams slipped the halter. At this point Jalal could have allowed himself to be led to the town's pastures, tethered to a stake where he would have grown fat until the day of his slaughter. Had this happened, Shams would never have returned. But instead the heifer broke the rope they had tied round his neck, and came in search of the Beloved. He chose God over his creatures, love before duty, the life in his heart before dead tradition.

'Yes, you passed your test.'

'And no?'

'You came in search of me, but you still have not found me.' The silhouette of Shams seemed to throb in the half light. 'The finding is all that remains.'

He stopped swaying, and turned to face Jalal. His eyes were hidden in shadow, but still Jalal felt his piercing gaze. 'I will never leave you again,' he said. 'And then I will.'

'When I am sad you make me happy,' Jalal said, half way between a laugh and a sob. 'And when I am happy you make me sad.'

Shams turned to face the wall again and Jalal rested his gaze on the old man's back. How could he be happy knowing that at any moment Shams could be snatched away again? He would be happy only if he could stop the dawn light growing any brighter through the shutters. Only if he could stay here forever, standing before his beloved friend, the shadows cast by the candle dancing for joy on the wall, would he be free from the fear of separation. Though he forbade his lips to form the words, his mind sent up the prayer to God: may I stay in this dream forever, Shams not in exile, but in a room of my own house.

'Come', Shams said, touching the floor beside him. 'It is better to pray than to sleep.'

•◆•

The brighter the light, the darker the shadow that it casts. And Shams of Tabriz burned brighter than any before him. Stand too close to him, and you would be burnt, turn your back on him and all you see is shadow – *your* shadow. For those who hated Shams – and there were many – it was themselves whom they hated. Those who heard nothing but dangerous blasphemy in his words were those who were afraid of their own shallow devotion and aberrant thought. Those who feared his wildness, feared their own wildness.

But for those with eyes to see, the black felt garb and scowling face were recognized for what they were – a disguise, beneath which the sun of divine grace blazed. Many loved Shams against their will, approaching him with uncertainty, keeping the warmth they felt in their hearts a secret. A few like Husam and Sultan Walad came closer, publicly avowing their allegiance to this man, casting their sense of propriety and fear and judgement into the flames. But none except Jalal had the courage to step into the flames themselves. *Love is the fire,* Shams had told him, *and our lower self is the firewood.* Jalal had thrown everything into the flames that Shams brought to him: his social position, his beliefs, his intellect, his fears. Uncertainty had gone; there was no hesitancy, no holding back – he was in the midst of fire, and beyond the touch of anyone. Shams had fulfilled his promise: he had destroyed Jalal.

Jalal tried to reassure those who had been insulted by Shams. 'Do not judge him as you would another person. One such as Shams cannot be measured by our standards. He is proud, yes, but it is the pride of the Self.'

Jalal begged his friend not to upset the people of Konya again, but Shams was unrepentant, and new complaints reached his ears almost daily.

'The common people are your responsibility, not mine,' the old dervish said. 'It is not my task to please them with sweet words and actions. I am the sun – how can I be blamed if the people get burnt? I am here to help *you*.'

Jalal laid his hand on his breast to convey his thanks. 'But can you not guard your tongue when you are in their presence? Your words are too honest for them – they sound painfully on untrained ears.'

'My words are not mine – they are from God.'

•◆•

A stray dog had given birth to a litter of pups in the alley behind the medrese, and Jalal had taken to bringing meat that the emir sent for him. The animal was thin and mangy, drained by her three pups, but Jalal still loved the dog. Husam accompanied him one day.

'You are worried,' Jalal said when he saw his friend's face. 'What is the reason?'

'It is Shams. He is so insulting. Even the most respected of your disciples he calls oxen and asses.'

Jalal tore a strip of meat from the bone and held it to the mouth of one of the pups. The animal nuzzled it, its eyes closed.

'And are you insulted?'

'Shams is good to me, but still I do not understand him. When he speaks, he seems to utter one blasphemy after another.'

The pup had given up nuzzling the meat, so Jalal offered it to another one.

'Mevlana, what are you doing?' Husam said gently. 'Such young pups cannot eat food like this.'

'And if one were to try?'

'He may choke and die.'

'But without food, the pup will die anyway.'

'It is the mother's job to feed her litter. If you want to save the pup, save the mother.'

Jalal removed the meat from the lips of the puppy and gave it to the bitch who snatched it from his hand. 'Shams is my meat sent from the palace. He has come for me – not for the people. Few can digest him.' He touched his friend's cheek with the back of his hand. 'Not even you, Husam. I am the mother dog, and you are my pups. Come to me, and drink my milk, but take nothing from the hand of Shams.'

Tears were in Husam's eyes, and his master smiled sadly. 'Have patience,' Jalal told him. 'We will all grow into our glory, and when we do, we will give thanks for the compassion that Shams has shown us.'

What image will do justice to the truth? Shams was the meat, Jalal the milk. Shams was the sun, Jalal the moon reflecting his light. Shams was the thorn, Jalal the rose. The townspeople could drink their master's milk, bask in his light, smell his perfume, but if they tried to take him in their hands, they would be pricked by the jealousy of the old man. And Shams would not withdraw his barbs: Jalal was his, and his alone. Jalal was counselled to distance himself from Shams, lest the dervish be driven out of the city as before, but there was nothing Jalal could do. He must give himself completely to his master. There was to be no more withholding, even if it cost Jalal everything.

Once again, Shams ordered the medrese to be closed. Finding the doors locked, his disciples came to their master's living quarters, but Shams stood in their way, arms folded across his chest. Protest was useless against such an unassailable guardian: reason had no place here, pleas fell on a stony heart. And so, again, Shams banished all but Jalal's closest disciples from seeing him.

If those who had known only the public face of Jalal saw him now, their fears would have been realized. In the darkened room where he sat with Shams, Jalal was more and more a drunken man. His vision may have been steady, but the eyes behind his eyes saw the room sliding and tilting. Those who engaged him in talk found a man who used words as if intoxicated. Breaking off in the middle of a sentence he would rise to whirl, or cry *Allah!*

and fall into a swoon. Though his legs walked without buckling, and though his hands performed the actions of a sober man, the spirit that impelled him was neither upright nor sober. He was flying, his body no longer the cage of his consciousness.

Those closest to Jalal begged Shams to release their master from this state, but the dervish sat in the shadows saying nothing, his bloodshot eyes glistening in the candle-light.

Sleep was banished for all in the household until exhaustion overcame them, and then they would wake an hour later to fall into the whirlpool of emotion that span between the two men.

Kerra Hatun was despairing. Her husband, so briefly hers again, was taken away from her once more. The food she brought him was eaten only when the knife was put in his hand; barely chewed, never tasted. His distracted gaze would pass over her, and she would weep and silently curse Shams for returning.

To see her husband, who loved her well and was well loved in return, pining for another person, even when that man was there – this was a goad even the most patient wife would kick against. Shams forbade her from their company when he was with Jalal and she complied, not from obedience, but because sight of them together pained her too much. The first time she saw Jalal tremble as he touched his friend's beard reminded her of his trembling when he had first seen her nakedness; she heard him groan as he looked into those fathomless eyes just as he had once groaned in love for her. 'You must separate yourself from him,' she whispered in her husband's ear late one night. 'Divorce yourself from him.'

'The marriage with a Master is eternal,' he replied. 'There can be no divorce.'

And so the fire burned even higher, and with the flames came poems. But the words which poured unbidden from Jalal were not a celebration. These desperate poems were an attempt at a remedy. Wet with emotion, each sought to extinguish the fire Shams had lit. As he turned in *sema,* words spilled from his lips and Husam, the scribe, caught them and stained parchment with them. No longer were the poems signed *Hamush*: every part of Jalal had disappeared in their creation; only one thing existed now: the sun of Shamsi Tabriz. There was only one name. His name.

Ask me who I am
and I will give the question back to you.
Who am I?
Tell me, stranger, who you see,
for I am lost to myself.
Like a drunkard forcing his eyes to still
the dancing words on the page
the fragments of myself dance before my gaze.
I am neither this nor that,

neither Muslim nor Jew,
neither sheikh nor disciple.
I have no tribe, no religion, no station.
All objects of all pasts
are less than a memory
– the dream of a dream.
Ask me my name and I will have to say 'Shams'
Ask me the name of my home and I will say
'in the house of the Beloved',
I have no name but His,
I have no home but His.
I know of nothing but Him.
I am nothing but Him.

There was no time any more. Every day was a lifetime for Jalal. Once he asked for a mirror to be brought to him and he gazed at his face, amazed that he was not yet an old man.

Shams had infinite patience, and no patience at all. Interrupted by a dervish seeking his blessing, he would fly into a rage, begrudging every second he spent away from Jalal. And yet hours would pass, running into days while he led his disciple inch by inch along the rocky path of the inner journey, never wavering for a moment from his duty.

And the journey had no end. Each bend in the road revealed another behind it, each summit was the foothill of another peak. At times Jalal thought he could bear it no longer, but then he would pass through his pain and exhaustion into unknown reserves.

Just when I think there is no more to give away
I find a storeroom inside myself,
Shams of Tabriz already there,
breaking the lock like a burglar
come to steal a treasure
of which I had no knowledge.

He is the lover come to steal my heart
and I am the drunken host
reckless with my possessions.
But I would gladly wake in the gutter,
clothes stained with wine,
for a single night of such generous proportions.

There was no understanding what was happening between Shams and Jalal, just one of two choices for those involved: to submit to their master's transformation or to rebel.

And there were many who rebelled. As the rumours began again, spreading through the town like a disease passed from mouth to mouth, hostility mounted. Two of his severest critics fell ill and Shams was blamed. A child was born deformed and died a few days later, a rabid dog was found outside the medrese. Whispers became murmurs, murmurs became spoken openly: Shams was a poison which needed to be drawn from the body of Konya.

Though the secrets of the future may be hidden from us, it does not require a seer to chart the course of a falling stone. Gravity will have its way – even fakirs who levitate must come down to earth. As resentment grew against Shams, the falling stone of the city's anger meant only one thing: confrontation.

Chapter Eleven

One day, a group of petitioners came to Mu'inuddin, the chief minister, to protest against Jalal's use of music and dance in religious ceremony, and begged him to outlaw such practices. The minister considered their suit and then decided to call Jalal to account for himself. The city was too divided in its opinion of their wayward imam for any decision to be satisfactory: some considered his behaviour scandalous, others were willing to tolerate actions from their Mevlana that they could not understand. Mu'inudddin was not prepared to upset either side; neither was he ready to pronounce against Jalal, for though Shams was held in almost universal disdain, Jalal was still the son of Baha Walad. Any decision against him would need the authority of more than a single man.

And so Mu'inuddin called all the learned people and men of piety to his palace for a religious debate. Muftis, imams and emirs; sheikhs, dervishes and scholars, all responded to his call. *They* would decide.

•◆•

The hall was full when Jalal arrived. The chief minister kissed his hand and welcomed him with fine phrases. Mu'inuddin was an ambitious man who knew the value of diplomacy. He did not care which way the debate went, but if he had to forbid this imam from dancing in the medrese, it was well to keep on the right side of his supporters.

A murmur of comment rose from the crowd of dignitaries when they saw who Jalal had brought with him. 'Here they come,' a pomaded gold merchant mocked. 'His ragged band of followers.'

His neighbour, a pious man agreed. 'Doubtless Jalal is a great saint, but we must save him from these people, drunkards and *kahin* every one of them.'

A dozen of his closest disciples took their places below the platform, scowling at the ill-concealed contempt that was shown them.

'At least that black dog Shams has been left tied up,' the merchant added.

A seat in the centre of the platform had been left empty for Jalal, and as he sat he gave blessings to those who greeted him. He folded his hands inside his sleeves and lowered his gaze, not looking at the faces before him. He was here because he had been ordered to attend. His days in the *mimbar* were over: philosophy was a beautiful trap: play with it for too long and your fingers would catch inside it. Satan, after all, was a better theologian than any of them.

Sultan Walad, seeing his father's gesture, sat on the floor in front of him. He felt the enmity directed at his back, but he kept his eyes fixed on his father's face, praying that he would not needlessly provoke the crowd.

The first speaker stood and formally bowed to the minister. He was a respected sheikh who had been openly critical of both Jalal and Shams, and his followers smirked at the worn figure of Jalal on the platform. 'The mystical dance you have instituted,' the sheikh began, addressing the crowd as much as Jalal, 'why should we not outlaw such forbidden practices?'

Jalal said nothing; indeed, it appeared that he hadn't even heard the question.

'If you say nothing,' the sheikh said coolly, 'we will have to conclude you are mad, just as some people are saying.'

Jalal still did not reply.

'*Are* you mad?' someone called out.

'The priests of Mecca said the Prophet Muhammad was mad,' Jalal said at last. 'If I am mad, it is in likewise manner.'

'And now he compares himself to the seal of the prophets!'

Jalal turned to the chief minister. 'My Lord, all my life I have obeyed the Holy Book. I am dust on the path of the Prophet Muhammad. Need I reply to such ill-conceived accusations?'

'But singing and dancing in the medrese,' the minister asked. 'Is this *sunnah*?'

Another man indicated he wanted to speak, so the sheikh sat down. 'I have read as many books as a mule can carry, the man said grandly, 'and in none of them is one line which allows music by holy law.'

'Then, my friend, you have read these books no better than the animal that bore them,' Jalal said quietly. There was laughter from Jalal's disciples, but he silenced them with a look. 'To understand music,' he added gently, 'you have to listen with your soul and not your ears.'

There was a mocking laugh from one of the ranks, and he jerked his head to find its source. 'Please, my friend – ', he saw the joker, with his grin and arrogant tilt of his head, 'there is more to gain here than we could possibly dream of.'

The man was immune to Jalal's sincerity. 'When the rebat plays, I just hear the creaking of doors,' he called out, turning to his friends for their approval.

'So do I, my friend. The doors of heaven opening.' Some of the assembly laughed, but Jalal did not smile. He appealed to the crowd with outspread hands. 'God bless the musicians and give their hands strength. Their songs have helped revive many a drooping heart – why should we not be grateful to them?'

The great mufti of Konya, sheikh Sadruddin stood up. He glared at the last speaker so there was no doubt of his disapproval. 'Do not listen to the small minds which adorn ignorance and call it learning,' Sadruddin said to the crowd. 'There is a *hadith* which tells us that an innovation introduced by a true lover of the prophets is the same as if it came from the prophets themselves.'

Assent was voiced, not just by the disciples of Jalal. There were many who loved Jalal still. At that moment there was a movement at the back of the hall, a sudden flutter of consternation. Shams had arrived. The debate was suspended while all eyes followed the ragged dervish as he made his way across the crowded floor to the platform, but when he neared the front, his way was barred by the disciples of the first sheikh. 'Take your seat where you belong – at the back,' one of them hissed.

Shams tried to find a place for himself, but at every empty seat, he was likewise barred from sitting. Husam rose and offered his seat to Shams, but the dervish shook his head and continued his search for an empty place. He wove his way through the crowd until he reached the back of the room, where he was allowed to sit in a draughty corner. Those who had no choice but to sit beside him turned away to their neighbours, ready to feign deafness if he spoke to them. But Shams was blazing with anger, his eyes fixed on the platform.

'Is Jalal such a true lover that he should have the authority for innovation?' a pomaded merchant called loudly. 'A lover, to be sure, but of what? Look at the object of his affection – a madman and heretic.'

'Well?' Mu'inuddin asked when Jalal offered no response.

'The word "affection" is a cup,' he said. 'I have an ocean of feeling for Shamsi Tabriz – I need a bigger container.'

His critics were hunting dogs rounding on a bear; they sensed the wound caused by insulting Shams, and when one of them stepped back, another lunged forward. 'What word shall we use? Infatuation?'

'Intoxication? Delusion?'

Sultan Walad could hold his tongue no longer. 'My father loves Shams. Let "love" be the word.'

A murmur of approval rose from the crowd: those who had known Jalal as a youth saw the same lineaments in his son.

'Still that is too small a word. *No* word, *no* container is large enough. Shamsi Tabriz cannot be contained by anything in God's creation,' Jalal said.

The first sheikh was on his feet. 'Beware Jalal of Rum. You are treading close to apostasy. The blasphemer Hillaj was stoned to death for seeking to raise a man to the level of God.'

'Hillaj was martyred for proclaiming "I am God"', Jalal replied. 'Was this blasphemy? Yes, if Hillaj had been Hillaj, but when he cried "I am God", he no longer existed. All that existed was God. Likewise, Shams no longer exists: he is annihilated. When you look at one such as Shams you do not see him – you see yourself. Beware attacking one who no longer exists, for you plunge your knife into your own body. When you lash out at a mirror, it is yourself who you attack.'

His words had found their mark, and the assembly was silent, waiting for what he would say next. He surveyed the faces before him, faces he had known all his life, and then he repeated the last words of Hillaj, the martyred saint as he approached the scaffold: 'Kill me, O my untrustworthy friends, for in my death there is my life.'

Jalal blinked the tears from his eyes and gazed at his friend. He suddenly knew what he had to do. A choice had to be made; these two bickering wives had to be parted once and for all. Jalal could be husband to either one, but not to them both. Saying nothing, he stood up and gathered his cloak about him.

There is often less distance between the highest and the lowest than between those who share the false camaraderie of equals. Jalal was the pinnacle of Konya, Shams the pariah, but with every step Jalal took from the despised platform, he came one step closer to himself. Jalal's eyes did not waver from those of his friend, and those seated on the floor had to lean to one side to let him pass.

Seyyid Sharif, seated next to the Governor, called loudly, 'Is not the chief seat of an assembly in the centre of the platform?'

Jalal paused. He spoke so quietly that those at the sides and back had to lean forward to hear. 'The chief seat is next to the Beloved.'

'Where is the Beloved?' he called sarcastically. 'We have all been searching for Him – please tell us so we can join you!'

'Are you so blind you cannot see Him?'

Jalal turned and walked to the back of the hall until he reached Shams. 'The God whom I have worshipped all my life is here in human form,' he said.

Jalal was deaf to the gasps and cries of outrage. He had made his choice.

•◆•

There had been no rain all summer. The sun scorched the fields day after day, baking the soil as hard as clay. During the noon sun, the white-washed buildings of the town dazzled the eye, the sky was as blue as the tiles of the medrese. The harshness of the plains heat softened at night into a heavy, airless blanket, driving the people of Konya onto their roofs to seek the merest breeze to dry their damp skin.

That night Jalal and Shams stood side by side on the city walls, watching the rising of the moon, now just a yellow smudge behind the dome of the Friday Mosque. The starlight was bright enough to reveal the broken lines of the flat roofs – the shapes of bodies on their sleeping pallets, clothes loosened against the sticky heat.

Jalal remembered the times he had walked these walls, sick with longing for sight of Shams, wailing at this very same moon. To think of it now brought feelings of shame to him: acting like a lovesick youth, pining for the touch of the Beloved, ready to throw away a life for the sake of a moment's embrace. And now, though Shams was here, separated from him by the slightest movement of his arm, there was no need to touch him. Jalal's love for Shams was not for this body, this presence, but for something else, something that Shams himself only represented. Jalal heard the words of the scriptures as clearly as if somebody had spoken them: *We have placed signs in the horizon and in yourselves.* Shams was not Shams – he saw it clearly now. The love that he felt for this dear friend who stood beside him was not love for another human being, but an emotion – no, it was a feeling beyond emotion, an *impulse* – whose true target was nothing but the One. God was in every pore of Shams; and in Jalal's worshipping of Shams, so God Himself was worshipped.

'It has been my duty to increase your longing,' Shams said, reading his thoughts, 'to draw it to a single point so that love for me is dearer than love for your next breath. Though love for the master is true love, it is only a beginning. Surrender to another person is not a great achievement – it is little more than a dog feels for its owner. That sort of love sounds no louder than this –' Shams clicked his fingers. 'Loving God, however, is different.' A distant rumble of thunder unfolded from beyond the mountains. A summer storm was coming.

'It is when the disciple loves God as he loves the teacher that progress is made. When all longing becomes a single longing, when all desires are but one desire – to be with God – *that* is an achievement.'

They turned to look at the lightning flickering in the distance. When Jalal gazed into his master's eyes he saw the lightning reflected there, as though two other worlds – one in each eye – were contained in each socket.

'I am afraid of this longing,' Jalal said. 'It will further anger the people, and they will drive you away.'

'If that is God's will, so be it. I am chaff in the wind – I cannot resist.'

A gust of cool air reached them, and it was as if God was offering reassurance. 'Let go', He was saying. 'It is safe.'

'One day I will not be here,' the old man murmured. 'It is then that God can claim the worship due to Him.'

'You must never leave me again!' Jalal begged. 'I cannot live without you.'

'I am your final obstacle. You must approach God alone.'

Jalal knew the truth of these words, but still he fought against them. 'Then stay as long as you can.'

'God will decide how long I stay.'

'Then I will wake the town!' Jalal cried. 'We must not miss a second of your presence here.'

Shams smiled. 'Wake them then – this is *your* duty.'

Jalal turned towards Mecca and knelt on the stone. 'Lord of Heaven and of Earth, for the love of your servant Shams of Tabriz, grant wakefulness to thy people.'

He touched his forehead on the ground, kept it there while he prayed for God's help.

Wake, don't sleep!
There is time enough in the grave
for dreaming.
Close not your eyes
against a beauty such as this.

Wake, don't sleep!
A beauty such as this but rarely comes

and even more rarely is seen.
People of Konya open your eyes
they will soon enough be closed in death.

A breeze passed over his exposed neck like a cool finger tracing a line between his tunic and his turban. Jalal shivered with pleasure and sat back on his heels. The smell of rain was in the air and he lifted his face to the sky. He inhaled the perfume of thunder, doubly delightful after the long weeks of summer drought. He felt the first spots of rain on his skin.

'*Allahu akbar! Allahu akbar!*' He raised his voice, calling again and again. '*Allahu akbar!*'

The rain fell in sheets. Suddenly and magnificently, rain was everywhere. Lightning crackled above them, the thunder so close and so loud his body was buffeted by the sound. Shams helped Jalal to his feet, water streaming down his face and off his beard. 'Look.' He pointed.

In the flashes of light they saw the people of Konya scuttling to collect their bedclothes, hurrying to escape the sudden downpour. Cries of alarm reached them on the city wall, shrieks of laughter as people hurried inside.

'Your prayer has been answered! Konya has awakened.'

Jalal turned to his friend, his tunic clinging to his skin, and kissed his hand in the Sufi manner. The old dervish enfolded Jalal in his robes and embraced him. His body shook, and Jalal thought that Shams was weeping, but when he was pushed away he saw his master was laughing. Head thrown back, mouth open, those strong white teeth made whiter by the gloom, Shams laughed and laughed and laughed.

Chapter Twelve

Two emotions fought for dominance in the heart of Alaeddin, the second son of Jalal: love for his father, and resentment towards Shams. Barely two years had passed since Shams had entered their lives, but time enough to lay low three generations of exalted status. Jalal, Baha Walad and Husain before him – great scholars all, princes of learning to whom kings bent their knee. Now the line had been broken by a single man, a wandering dervish with no lineage, no authority, no learning.

The convocation at the minister's palace had resolved nothing; the meeting had ended in confusion, no decision having been made. Alaeddin had hoped Shams would have been banished, or at least forbidden from seeing his father, but no such action had been taken, and the threats of such action had been laughed at by the dervish. When the wooden bolt slid across their cell door, the two men entered a country in which foreign laws applied.

'This man is leading your father astray,' his friends told him. 'Destroying his prestige as well.'

And mine too, Alaeddin thought bitterly. For every public outburst of his father, the son paid dearly. To see his father, once a great man who had steered the world from his pulpit, shaped government, dispensed justice, broadcast wisdom – reduced to this: a man, barely sane, who would rather play with children in the street than talk with sages, a man who saw no distinction between Muslim and Jew, a man who would as readily bow to a beggar woman as a sheik. Were they to be blamed if honour was not afforded, that respect was withdrawn? At first Alaeddin had been alarmed by this ragged dervish, and then felt sadness to see his father brought so low, then anger, then finally, resolution.

Alaeddin was a fiery young man, used to speaking his mind, but though others railed openly against Shams, Alaeddin guarded his heart and his tongue. He would be responsible for no rumour which could hurt his father; no gossip would pass from his lips that could return to the house of Jalal. But if the elders could not take action, Alaeddin thought bitterly, I will have to myself. Feelings and words had little impact in this world, he told himself – it was action that was needed. He would confront

Shams of Tabriz, endure that withering glance, throw water of disdain on the fire of his anger. Konya must be rid of the dervish.

Shams afforded him an audience for one reason only: he was the son of Jalal. 'There are two sides to everything, and two sides to sons,' he told the youth that stood before him in his cell. 'The good son, and the bad son. Sultan Walad is the good son. You are the bad.'

Alaeddin stiffened as though the blow had been a physical one. He tried to look at the older man, but his glance darted everywhere other than to the face of Shams. Staring at the ground by his feet, he spoke the prepared lines. 'My father has taught me that respect for elders follows after respect for God. It is because I respect God first, that I say these words –'

He could feel the eyes of Shams on him, but he dared not look up. A wave of nausea passed over him, and he felt his body sway. Suddenly all his words left him, and his mind was blank. Just standing before Shams was enough to drain him of resolve.

'I know your thoughts,' Shams sneered. 'Your petty ambition and childish rage. There is something here that you will never understand. Nothing can make me leave the side of your father.'

'We don't want you here,' Alaeddin countered, his anger rising. He dared to raise his head and look at Shams. 'You are destroying my father!'

'You presume to judge me?' Shams shouted. He leapt to his feet and started beating the youth around the ears. Snatching up his staff, he then struck Alaeddin across the shoulders. Alaeddin cried out in alarm, his arms raised to fend off the blows. Shams kicked open the door and bundled the young man from his room, pushing him into the courtyard until he fell. Alerted by the noise, people came running.

'How can you turn against me again?' he shouted at them. 'Do you not see the gifts I am bringing? Are you so stupid you see only my rags?'

He turned and strode back into his room, slamming the door behind him. Alaeddin watched him from the ground, a new look in his eyes – hatred.

Jalal soon heard of the quarrel. Shams came to him, storming and spitting venom. 'They are dogs and sheep!' he complained. 'I swear I will leave this city again. I will disappear so completely this time that nobody will ever find me again.'

Jalal tried to placate him, and then called Alaeddin and ordered him to apologise to the dervish. For the first time in his life, Alaeddin defied his father. 'Can't you see what's happening to you?' he said. 'Every time you go out in public you make a fool of yourself. People are laughing at you.'

Jalal looked at his son and saw that he had become a man. When had this happened? It was only yesterday that he was a child, and now a wispy beard clung to his chin, and his forearms rippled with muscles. Jalal was ashamed of himself: he had been so blinded by the light of Shams that all else had been invisible.

'I am sorry for your pain,' Jalal said. 'But I will not change. We must all follow our path, and this is mine.'

•◆•

That night Jalal's tiny chamber was filled as usual with those who came for evening worship. Kneeling at the front, Jalal led the prayers, his beautiful voice calling with such passionate longing, that even now, after twenty years of marriage, Kerra Hatun felt awe. Kneeling with the women at the back of the room, she scanned the figures before her: Sultan Walad, so like his father, Husam kneeling beside him, Shams next and then two other disciples. Alaeddin's place was empty.

Kerra Hatun had also heard of Alaeddin's fight with Shams, the subsequent exchange between father and son, the argument with his brother that followed. Alaeddin had come to her, tearful and angry, and told her everything. Watching him pace the room before her, hands clenching and unclenching, Kerra had seen him as Jalal had. No longer the child prone to tantrums, this was a man enraged. She had seen his resentment building for months: not just against the old dervish, but also his elder brother, Sultan Walad, the favourite of Shams. Now a line had been crossed: he had publicly condemned Shams, defied his father, fought with his brother. She had begged Alaeddin to calm himself, not do anything rash, but he had ignored her.

Kneeling now at the back of the room, her mind too restless to follow the prayers, Kerra was frightened: something terrible was about to happen. Alaeddin had left in a rage, and now all she could see were these vulnerable backs, bowed before her as though offering themselves in sacrifice.

When the room emptied after the prayers, Jalal was left, his forehead still resting on the ground. When he finally sat up and turned, she knew from his look that he failed to recognize her.

'Husband,' she said. 'Others have spoken to you, and you have paid no attention. Now it is for me to speak.'

He indicated for her to continue.

'Unless you put distance between yourself and Shams,' she said, 'other people will do it for you.'

Jalal pondered the words and then nodded. 'I know that many people hate him, but what can I do? I am part of Shams, he is part of me. How can I distance myself from him? I can cut off my arm if I despise it, but Shams is more deeply interfused than that. Shams is my life blood – separate me from that and I will be no more.'

'This is madness. You will not die without Shams.'

'I will.'

Kerra Hatun studied her husband's face as though she was seeking to remember every line and pore, as though she expected never to see him again. She rose and paused at the door. 'I am frightened for Alaeddin, what he might do.'

'All is in the hands of the Almighty,' Jalal said. 'Trust Him.' Kerra left and Jalal took up his quill and wrote:

There is nothing I can do.
The One beckoned me from the garden of reason,
and I vaulted its walls.
Now I find myself falling
a thousand, thousand fathoms
and still no sign of landing.

He put down the quill and closed his eyes in prayer. He would gladly take all suffering on himself, his wife's pain, his son's anger, the confusion of his disciples, but no life could be lived for another person. 'Merciful God,' he murmured, 'comfort those who suffer, encourage those who fear. The only ground under our feet is that which is imagined. We are all falling, whether we know it or not. Lord God, please guide us in our falling.'

It was that night when they heard a knock on the door. Jalal and Shams were sitting together in silence, both waiting and yet not knowing for what they waited. A voice was heard from outside, 'Hazreti Shams, a dervish has come to pay his respects to you. He begs that he may kiss your hand before going on his way.'

Shams slowly got to his feet. He placed his right hand on his breast and bowed to Jalal. When he opened the door, the draught caught the candle flame and shadows leapt across the walls like demons.

Shams turned in the doorway and Jalal reached a hand out to him. He wanted to beg him not to go, warn him of some unknown danger, but no words came to him.

The door closed behind his friend. Though there was no sound but the wind, nothing to see but the bare walls, the room was filled with the presence of Shams. There was a perfume in the air, the scent of God.

Jalal prostrated himself on the floor, a verse from the Qur'an springing to his lips. 'The sun, the moon and the stars are subject to His command. Know well that it is in His power to command and create. How great is the glory of God, Lord of the Heavens.'

Chapter Thirteen

Shams did not return to his cell that night. Jalal waited for him, poised like a man on the very pinnacle of a mountain, balancing on one foot at the top of the world, wind gusting and threatening to spill him over, yet keeping his balance. When the candle guttered and was extinguished, he waited in the dark. When the *muezzin* called before dawn, he made no move. When the sun had risen, he stirred, taking the first step off the peak, back into the warm air of his emotions. There was no word to attach to the sensations that movement brought.

He called Sultan Walad to his room.

'What is wrong, father?'

Jalal forced himself to shape the words: 'Go and seek Shams and bring news of his whereabouts to me.'

It had been no empty threat. Shams had been speaking the truth when he said he would leave. Though Jalal knew that Shams had flown, he still needed to hear the words from others. And so servants searched the medrese, the mosque, the market, and returned with the news that Shams had not been found.

What manner of bird are you
to so completely fly away?
Have you left no feather I can brush to my face –
a memory of flight if not flight itself?

Where have you gone?
Would that I had the eye of the sun
to follow your course over the horizon.
Were I the wind under your wing
holding you aloft, even as you escape me.

Shams, my sun, the centre of my world
I am grounded, a shot bird,
a partridge, a pheasant, a pigeon.
Before I was an eagle
but now there is too much sky without you.

Had there been no ink, Jalal would have dipped the quill in his blood, used his own flayed skin for parchment. Jalal banished visitors to his cell. He could bear no company other than his writing tools, bear no sound except the scraping of the quill. He wrote without pause, day and night. He slept at the writing stool, weeping in his dreams only to wake and weep again.

I am not the writer, I am the pen.
The hand that holds me belongs to another.
I am not the musician, I am the flute.
The lips against mine belong to Shams.

The poems that poured from him were no balm, they were the wind on flames making the blaze reach higher, burn hotter. He tore his clothes in his distraction, ate only when Kerra placed food in his mouth. The doctors came, prescribed poppy juice, but he flung it at the wall.

Let no one sleep until my love is found.
Banish dreams from the house.
Stay wakeful till dawn
lest the Beloved comes in the night.

Throughout each night a candle burned at his window, another one on his writing stool as poem after poem flowed from his pen like tears from his face.

And when the pain became too great, he rose and whirled, burning himself away until the figure became incandescent, a flaming pillar of agony. He ate nothing, he drank nothing; any normal man would have fallen exhausted, but he whirled and cried and sang with a strength which could come from only one source. Jalal was sustained by nothing other than God's grace; the only things stopping him falling to the ground were the hands of angels.

Friends, tell me he was more than a dream
tell me he walked in a body,
much like other men.
Call the town out to ask
whether such a one ever lived.
I have his belt here, his shoes worn at the toe.
His feet touched here, his waist girdled by this rope.
He did live, my friends – did he not?
The memory of him eating in my house,
sleeping on this pallet,
the warmth I still feel on my cheek
from sitting so close to him –
am I deluded?
Surely he was here,
a man of flesh and blood,
my beloved, my friend?

This was not some temporary love-sickness, a mind infatuated with a product of its own making; this was a physical pain. It was there in Jalal's every movement: the writhing of a severed worm, the flapping of a fish out of water, the groan as a tree was felled. Shams was no companion whose absence would turn to nostalgia and fond memories, he was as much part of Jalal as his own soul. And there was no sedative, no remedy, nothing that could assuage the pain of being separated from himself.

•◆•

That single night when Shams went missing had changed everything and everybody, and no one more than Alaeddin. Now he kept his distance from his father. His face was troubled, and more than once he was heard arguing with his brother.

Now Shams had gone, the elders of Konya looked forward to their imam returning to his senses. Jalal had been away a long time, lost in the foreign country of this *qalandar*; now, surely, he would regain his sanity, return to the medrese, wear his father's cap once more. Husam was questioned about his master's health, but what could he say? Who had ever witnessed such a malaise before? He went to Jalal and asked for a message for the people, and returned with these words: 'I was raw before I met Shams. Then I was cooked. Now I am burning.'

And so he was. Jalal was aflame with rage against God. Husam quaked to hear his master talk thus. 'How could you do this to me?' Jalal would cry. 'I have given you everything, I have devoted myself to you, and this is the reward I receive – to be abandoned! What is my crime that I should be thus punished? I loved too much! I have worked hard, studied, fasted, meditated, denied myself, and what do I get? The illiterate blacksmith who has never ventured beyond the city walls is happier than I am. I am condemned to wandering – I have no home any more, in my stupidity I destroyed it.'

'Why did His hand have to land on my shoulder?' Jalal would demand of Husam. I do not want this. I want none of it. I want to rest in oblivion. I want to be a dog sleeping in the sun.'

'I should have lived my life as others do. I should have blocked my ears to the call, stayed at home, followed the easy path from my house to the medrese and back. It was God who made me cut my own path through the wilderness, picking my way through rocks, scaling sheer cliff faces, and never did He give me any rest. Now I find I have ruined my life for Him, and there is no rebuilding it.'

In a drunken state
I burned my professor's chair
my sleeping pallet
the home in which I lived.
Now there is nowhere for me to sit,
or lie, or rest,

just smouldering remains.
You made me burn the forests
and carpenters and all their tools.
Now look at me –
even if I wanted, there could be no home any more.
I don't even have my clothes –
you made me throw them into the fire.
And all the cotton fields have gone,
all the looms, all the cloth merchants.
Now look at me –
I am more naked now than when I came into the world.

Jalal forced Husam to listen. 'Perhaps the unbelievers are right,' he would say, '– that God cares nothing for us, that the life of Jalal is no more important than the life of his mule, that the spiritual journey is barren and aimless, leading the traveller deeper into the desert where it is only by chance he finds an oasis, or by chance dies of thirst.

'If God is so compassionate, so merciful, then why are we surrounded by suffering? If God delivers us the events of our lives, why is He so indiscriminate? Why does the sinner suffer no more than the saint? Why do the innocent perish along with the guilty?

'There is no escape, Husam. I look at my sons and see more links in the manacles that bind them to this world. Even as babies they were condemned, chained to their bodies, their little minds, their fate. Now as men they are no closer to being free – their chains have just grown thicker. I see Sultan Walad with my mark on his forehead, the mark of a man condemned to follow God. Alaeddin, no less loved by me for the mark he bears: that of the world, following his appetites and passions, condemned to eat and drink only to hunger and thirst again. Is there no end to this? Will they too have sons who are born into chains? Will only death relieve our suffering – or not even then?'

Jalal took his weeping and ranting to the marketplace. Crowds gathered, excited at first to see their master, but soon shocked by what they heard.

'Try to control yourself,' he was advised.

'I have sought control all my life,' he would cry in reply. 'Now the river can take me wherever it will.'

He was beyond caring what others thought. He fell into the dust and rolled like a madman. He tried to tear his clothes from his body, stopped only by his disciples who were cast into disarray to see their master like this.

The only salve to Jalal's wound was to whirl. He would turn on one spot for hours, washing his mind clear of everything but the moment, seeking to bring his death forward, to die before he died. Only for these moments out of time was the heavy crown of consciousness lifted, and Shams was no longer absent because there was no longer time; no longer distant because there was no longer space. But even whirling must come to an end, the crown be taken back again. And with consciousness came the cry of suffering.

Sultan Walad could endure seeing his father's pain no longer. 'You must let Shams go, father. He is never coming back.'

'Where is he? You know where he is?'

'I cannot lie.'

Jalal threw his arms up. 'Praise be to God! Tell me, quickly – where is he?'

Sultan Walad saw the desperation in his father's eyes and his resolve faltered. 'He is in Damascus,' he said quietly.

'I knew it!' Jalal cried triumphantly. 'We will go immediately.'

Chapter Fourteen

Sultan Walad had never felt so alone. The journey to Damascus took sixty days: just himself and his father and two mules, a caravan so poor that bandits themselves might take pity on them. There was almost nothing of his father left: there was no conversation along the way, no words of encouragement or comfort or thanks, nothing except *Shams*. Hour after hour the son rode behind his father, days passing with barely a word. As he watched his father's back he wrestled with his dilemma: should he speak the truth about Shams? Many times he decided to tell his father, and each time he quailed at the thought. I will wait until we are in Damascus, he decided, or perhaps back in the safety of Konya where somebody else can tell him the truth.

Sultan Walad did not know if he loved Shams or hated him. Everything was in place before the dervish had come into their lives: Jalal was father to Sultan Walad, Alaeddin was his brother. Now his brother was his enemy, and he found himself thrust into manhood, protecting his own father as though it was *he* who was the parent and Jalal was the child. And his first act as a parent? To lead his hapless father on a journey which could only end in disappointment. Not a day passed that Sultan Walad did not curse himself for putting the idea in his father's head. What could they possibly find in Damascus other than more pain? If Jalal was not fully destroyed now, the truth would ensure his final destruction.

But though the outer journey was no less arduous than the inner one, the young man was keen to the privilege of being the son of such a father. Everything about Jalal was great: his wisdom, his passion, his endurance – even his suffering. Though he often agreed with his father's detractors, believing that Shams had become a sickness for him, sometimes Sultan Walad glimpsed the adoration for what it was: not the love for a man, but the love for God; not a seeking to possess, but a being possessed. At times like this, the young man stood in awe of his father, this stranger who shone as much with grace as with pain. And when he saw this, he bent his knee again in gratitude to Shams. He just prayed that his father would survive the ordeal.

Chapter Fourteen

Damascus was a crossroads, a town accustomed to travellers who sought anonymity, and the two pilgrims from Anatolia entered the city unnoticed. Only now did Sultan Walad see the condition of his father: unkempt and dusty, his beard shot through with grey, his eyes glittering, his cloak ragged. Nobody would have taken him for the famous imam of Konya, Jalal-uddin son of Baha Walad. He looked like any other dervish. He looked like Shamsi Tabriz.

Jalal would not wash or pray, or even seek lodgings. The journey had been long, and there was no reason to prolong it. 'Take me to the Friend,' he said.

Another opportunity to tell the truth, but again Sultan Walad could not bring himself to utter the words. He led his father through the market to the courtyard where he had first found Shams playing chess. A noisy group of traders was sitting in the shade where Shams had sat with the Frankish monk. The traders were drinking wine and gambling with dice, too busy to notice the two dusty travellers.

'Which is his door?'

'I do not know, father.'

'This one?' He pointed to the first door.

'No.'

'This one?' Jalal lifted his fist to knock.

'No.'

'Tell me, son, or else I will have to break every door down.'

Sultan Walad could bear it no longer. 'He is gone, father. He is *gone!*'

'Where?'

'He is *dead*.'

Jalal stared at him as though the word was familiar but still not understood. 'Dead?' he said at last.

'Yes.'

'Liar!'

'It is true!'

'Which is his door?'

'It was this one.'

Jalal ran towards the door and tried to open it, but it was bolted. He hammered on the wood with his fists, trying to break it open.

'Hoi!' The landlord came running.

'Open the door! Let me see him!'

Sultan Walad tried to quieten his father, tugging at his arm to lead him away, but he was ignored. 'The sun of Tabriz is staying here. Let me see him!'

The gamblers paused to watch the spectacle: there was a more interesting game here than dice. Jalal continued to hammer on the door, demanding entrance, and the landlord, afraid for the safety of his property, was trying to wrestle him away. Alarmed at the indignity his father was suffering at the hands of such a man, Sultan Walad tried to subdue the landlord.

'Hassan!' the landlord shouted.

A stable boy came running. He took Jalal's other arm and, together with the landlord, they steered the gesticulating man out of the courtyard and then pushed him into the street.

'Drunken idiot!' the landlord shouted after him. 'Clear off!'

The traders laughed and jeered, and Sultan Walad led his father to a fig tree and tried to make him sit down, but Jalal was too agitated. He raised his head to the sky and sang:

Who dares say the immortal one has died?
Who dares say that the sun of hope has set?
An enemy of the sun has climbed onto the roof
Closed his eyes and declared the sun has set.

He would not believe it. How *could* he believe it? How could Shams die, and not the whole world die with him? Where the earthquakes, the falling stars? Where the sound of rending as heaven and earth are torn asunder?

'It is not so, son,' he groaned. 'Tell me you are lying.'

'Father, you frighten me. Have you forgotten everything you were taught?'

Jalal grasped his son's hands, squeezing them so hard that Sultan Walad flinched. 'Teach me. I am completely lost.'

'Remember Umar.'

'The Second Caliph? Yes. Tell me quickly.'

Sultan Walad spoke through his tears. It frightened him to see his father thus, teetering on the edge of madness. 'He would not accept the death of a beloved friend, either.'

'Cut off the arms and legs of anyone who tells me Muhammad is dead,' Jalal murmured. He knew now how the friends of the Prophet had felt when he died. The sky had fallen.

'And what did Hazreti Abu Bakir tell him?'

Jalal was back in the caravanserai with his father, searching his memory for the correct answer, but his grief had robbed him of all his learning, and the more he searched, the more the answer receded.

'If you have been worshipping Muhammad,' Sultan Walad began, prompting his father.

It suddenly came to him. 'If you have been worshipping Muhammad then know that Muhammad is dead. But if you have been worshipping God, then know that God is –' His voice cracked and he covered his face with his hands.

Sultan Walad finished for him. 'Know that God is living, and never dies.'

Chapter Fourteen

Jalal scrubbed at the tears that sprang from his eyes. His fingers, sooty from that morning's campfire left black streaks down his face. He looked up and his glance fell on a man whitewashing his walls with a bucket and paint stick. Leaping to his feet, he ran to the man and snatched the stick from him and then hurried back to the courtyard.

Before anyone could stop him he began daubing the name of Shams on the door. The traders roared with laughter at this fresh sport, and the landlord ran back to see the cause of the commotion. Seizing the stick from Jalal, he began beating him over the head and back with it. The stable boy joined in, kicking and pushing the figure. Sultan Walad tried to hurry his father from the courtyard, but they stumbled against the table of the traders, spilling some of their drink. The mocking laughter of the men turned to shouts of outrage. One of them spat at Jalal, another stood up and drew his dagger from its sheath.

Jalal pounced on the blade, wrenching it from the man's hand. The men stepped back, but Sultan Walad knew they had nothing to fear. It was to his own heart that Jalal levelled the blade.

'Father! Stop!' he cried.

'I cannot do more than die,' Jalal said, aghast, watching the dagger being taken from his hands and thrown to one side. He grasped the hands of the traders whose knife he had snatched. 'Who was responsible?' he demanded. 'Who killed the sun?'

The man pushed Jalal away, afraid of this madness, and so Jalal turned to his son.

'Who?'

'Does it matter who held the knife? There were many.'

'Give me the names of his murderers.'

'Please father, do not make me say more.'

'Tell me!'

'Your son, Alaeddin.'

Jalal fell to his knees, hands held to his head. He wailed so loudly that his grief shrivelled the anger of the drunken traders. Again and again the wail was torn from his bosom, an uncanny sound, more animal than human. He beat his chest and face, threw himself in the dust, screamed into the bowels of the earth.

It was the landlord who spoke first. 'Get this man out of here,' he growled at Sultan Walad.

A man who had been watching from the street came into the courtyard and helped lift Jalal to his feet. Together with Sultan Walad, they steered the sobbing man back to the fig tree and made him sit down. The stranger did not ask the cause of the man's distress, but just patted the shoulder of Sultan Walad and left.

Jalal slept under the tree, his son watching over him as he murmured in his sleep, cried out once. A stray dog came close, and though Sultan Walad tried to shoo it away, it only cowered and crept closer until it lay with its head on Jalal's arm.

Chapter Fourteen

When his father woke at dusk he questioned Sultan Walad about the murder. There was relief in shedding such an onerous secret, and Sultan Walad told him all that he knew. Seven assassins, each armed with a knife. Jalal silently wept as his son related their names, each one a disciple, each one well loved. Shams had died without a struggle, not even raising his arms to defend himself. They had thrown his body down a well, and sworn an oath of secrecy.

'They thought they were doing good, father,' Sultan Walad pleaded when his father said nothing. 'They love you so much, and were so afraid that Shams would destroy you. Please forgive them.'

'And Alaeddin?'

'He came to me in the night and confessed what he had done. He wanted to tell you, but I forbade him. He took me to the well and showed me the body of Shams. He was so ashamed and grief-stricken I had to stop him throwing himself down after Shams.

'We pulled the body out, and washed it together, and then buried it in the college grounds. He rests beside your father. Forgive me for not telling you.'

Jalal suddenly stood up. 'We will return to Konya immediately.' His face was drawn and pale, and he wouldn't look at Sultan Walad.

'But father, it will be night soon, and a storm is coming.'

The setting sun was orange and smudged with an approaching sand storm.

'God is in the desert. He has something for me,' Jalal said simply.

They led their two mules to the city walls, ignored by the hurrying people as they covered windows and doorways against the approaching storm, leading sheep and goats inside for safety.

The two had only walked a short distance from the city walls when Sultan Walad stopped. It would be dark soon, and the moon was covered. The wind had already picked up, and a fine dust blew into their eyes. 'Father, this is madness. We must seek shelter.'

For a moment Jalal seemed to come to his senses. He surveyed the twilight, hearing for the first time the slashing of the wind through the palm trees. 'Run, my son!' he cried. 'Go back to the city.'

But it was too late. The storm was upon them. The mules turned with their rumps to the wind and Sultan Walad crouched in their lee, but Jalal pushed forward.

Sultan Walad left the animals and caught up with his father. 'Where are you going?' he shouted above the gale. 'You can only become lost in the dark.'

'I am already lost. God has abandoned me.'

'Do not talk like that!'

'God is against me!' Jalal shouted, sand stinging his face. 'Even the wind is against me!'

Sultan Walad forced his father to stop. He seized him by the head and shouted into his ear. 'Do not curse the wind, for it derives from the breath of the All Merciful. It was *you,* father, who told me this.'

Suddenly Jalal realized that it was not the wind who was against him, not *God,* but the other way round. It was *he* who had set his face against God. He realized that he could turn so the wind was at his back, pushing him forward, no longer resisting his movements. If he did not know where he was going, then why insist on forging into the face of the storm? He need not fight any more. He need not insist that he knew how things should be. He could accept the death of Shams. He could say yes instead of no. He could surrender.

It took nothing to turn around, just a simple twist of the body and Jalal found himself bowled forward with the snapped palm fronds and pieces of straw. He laughed as the wind tried to lift him, stumbling as his legs failed to keep up with the speed the wind insisted. He did not know where he was going, just following the will of the wind as it pointed him this way and that, staggering sometimes, falling only to rise again, the wind at his back pushing him forward into the glorious unfolding of life. He realized now that he had never fully surrendered to God, that until now he had always retained some of his personal struggle, that never had he said of everything in his life, Yes Lord, this too I give to you.

And so he span and staggered and stumbled, just one more piece of debris caught by the wind, obscured by the thickness of the sand in the air and the darkness of the night.

There was no telling for how long he was bowled along by the wind before he found himself pressed against something unresisting. His hands explored in the darkness, and he felt the stone bricks of a wall. He followed the wall with his fingers until he found the door, and then he lifted the latch and was inside.

It was so different here. He had been blind and deaf outside, and now his senses returned to him as something marvellous and rare. He looked around as though at any moment his wondrous sight may be taken away once more.

A low ceiling with bare beams. A single oil lamp. A man sitting, his back against the bare wall. A woman hurriedly veiling her face. A crib. A low table. Two clay goblets, a brass dish catching the light. A bleat coming from a young goat in the corner.

'*Assalaam alaikum,*' the man said. 'Peace be upon you.' He did not seem surprised at the sudden entrance of Jalal. 'Come inside, brother.'

'*Alaikum assalaam,*' Jalal replied, bowing. 'And on you be peace.'

The man gestured to the floor, inviting his unexpected guest to sit on a rush mat. Jalal lowered himself gently as though he was in a dream and any sudden movement might waken him.

'You have brought light,' the man said, giving the formal Arab greeting.

'The light is yours,' Jalal replied, giving the formal reply.

There was a long pause as they listened to the wind. 'A bad storm, brother,' the man said at last.

'Yes.'

'It will be over soon.'

'God willing.'

Another long pause as the woman bent over the fire and stirred a pot of food.

'Tell me, brother,' the man said, 'Where is the other man, and the two mules?'

Jalal realized that this was the person who had helped him from the courtyard. 'The man is my son. God will protect him.'

The wife of the shepherd ladled food onto two wooden plates. She gave one plate to Jalal and the other to her husband.

It was a thin barley gruel, seasoned with salt and butter.

'I am a poor man,' the shepherd said, 'but what I have is yours.'

Jalal suddenly realized how hungry he was. He ate as though in a dream. Each spoonful of gruel was a miracle. Jalal watched the hand that lifted the spoon to his mouth, felt the warmth of the gruel on his lips, tasted the salt on his tongue, and with each mouthful he was awestruck at the divine improbability that this grain, fed by sunlight and water should be entering the body which sat beside him – *his* body. He marvelled at the divine plan that should allow the transformation of grain to flesh, husk and kernel to thought and spirit. Not just for him, but for every creature in the universe – animals, plants, every living being – *everything* was in constant flow, taking in, giving out, sustained by the inexhaustible and loving God. But not just His creatures – *everything* was vibrant with life: not just the goat, the smiling man, the black eyes of his wife watching them, but every object in this perfect world was radiant with energy: the walls of the room pulsating in the lamplight, the stones under his feet, the stalks of straw, the sickle in the corner.

'Do you not like the food, effendi?' the host asked. He had eaten his food in the time it had taken Jalal to swallow five mouthfuls.

Jalal realized the bowl was forgotten in his lap, and looked down in surprise to see the food was almost untouched. He began eating again, though he was no longer hungry. His movements were slow, the actions of a man unfamiliar with the customs of materialism. The food, though, was performing its magic, for Jalal felt the strength flowing back into his body. He finished the bowl and thanked his host.

The shepherd politely questioned Jalal about his business in Damascus and Jalal found himself relating the entire story of Shams: the first meeting in the market when Shams had taken his hand and spun Seyyid Burhan in his arms; Shams stopping his mule on the way to the medrese and asking his question about who was the greater – Muhammad or Beyazid Bestami; the scene in the medrese as Shams threw the books into the pool and then brought them out again dry. He told them of his love for his friend, and the opposition from the people of Konya, how Shams was driven away to Damascus, how Sultan Walad brought him back, only for him to disappear a second time.

'And where is your friend now?' the shepherd asked.

'He is dead, murdered by my second son.'

The woman gasped from under her veil, but the shepherd did not seem surprised. 'Such things happen,' he said.

The simple reply of this pious man touched Jalal's heart. 'I cannot pay you for the food,' Jalal said. 'I seem not to have my money pouch.' He studied his fingers, and felt around his neck. 'Nor do I have any rings or jewels I can give you. All I can give you is a story.'

The shepherd clapped his hands, indicating for his wife to sit beside him. 'Pay attention, wife. We have a great imam here.'

Jalal paused, waiting for the spirit of a story to come to him. He had no prepared tale; he was not a storyteller with a bag full of adventures and parables, he was a blind pilgrim who found his way through the landscape by touch alone.

'A man knocked at his friend's door,' Jalal began. '"*Who's there?*" the voice came from inside. "*It's me! Let me in.*" "*Go away,*"' the voice said. "*This table is for cooked food only. There is no place here for raw people.*" The man dearly wanted to share the company of his friend, and he was willing to do anything. "*How can I prepare myself?*" the poor man asked. "*How can I become cooked?*"'

Jalal looked at the shepherd and his wife as though they might supply the answer. The man nodded for him to continue. "*The only thing that can cook you and save you from yourself is the fire of being apart from me.*"

The shepherd laughed, thinking it was to be a funny story, but his wife shushed him.

'This was the last thing the wretched man wanted to hear, but he was desperate, so he went away for a year, and sure enough, he was burned by the separation. When he was good and cooked he returned. He paced up and down beside his friend's house, nervous that he might say the wrong thing again. Anyway, he knocked and his friend called out: "*Who is it?*"'

Jalal paused again, and again the shepherd nodded for him to continue. 'Something happened to the man just then. Hearing his Beloved's voice, all thoughts of himself left his head. The answer came out of his mouth as though somebody else had spoken: "*You, my dear friend, YOU are at the door!*" The door was flung open, and the friend stood there. "*Come on in, since you are myself. There is no room in this house for both you AND me.'"*

The shepherd waited for more, and then smiled when it was clear that Jalal had finished. 'A strange tale, brother.'

Indeed it was. Jalal now saw that to enter the house of God, he needed to be destroyed. Two could not share the space of one. Not until he had stopped searching would he find that which he sought.

When the searching was over, then the traveller could see what had been the truth all along: that he was here, in these circumstances, and now, in this time, and that all notions of 'self' and 'other' were just inventions. Not resisting this reality was the doorway to God's heart. A simple stepping back from judgement was enough to deliver what Jalal had sought; for suddenly the veils had dropped from Jalal's heart, and he saw how beautiful everything was. Not just the glowing colours in the light of the oil lamp, the kind faces of his hosts, but *everything.* It was all beautiful: the simplicity of this hut, the chapped and blistered feet of the shepherd, the wind moaning through the rafters. All glorious, all joyous. Everything towards which Jalal had levelled a 'no': his own shortcomings, the death of Shams, the absence from God – these things became gloriously *Yes!* All were the will of God, a God who loved his creatures more than they could possibly love him. How had he not seen this before?

He was surrounded by God. Above, below, behind, in front – there was a perfect fit: the precise point that his own body ended, so the body of God began. But even his own body was God: every cell within him was alive with divinity. There was no space left: not even the sharpest blade could pass between himself and God, between God as the ground and God as the foot. Everything was testimony to God's abundance. Every event – even the body of Shams thrown down a well – *all* was God. God weeping, God laughing.

There was nothing other than God. Every breath that Jalal took was vibrant with God, every sound was brought from its origin to Jalal's ear, hurried by the hand of God. There was no need to pursue God, He was pursuing His own creation. Every step Jalal took towards God, God would take a hundred towards him. When Jalal came walking, God came running.

And now he experienced an emotion that he hadn't felt for years, an unfamiliar feeling, dimly recalled and now suddenly vivid: he felt *happy*. Something broke inside him, and he found himself weeping for the way in which he had deprived his soul of happiness, for the unrequired hardships he had demanded, for the exile he had imposed on himself. For years, for *ever,* God had been here waiting. The friend had not needed to be sought, but discovered. The treasure Jalal had been looking for all his life was not in some distant land, but in the foundations under the house in which he lived, a house which needed to be destroyed in order to reach the treasure.

He had sought God in the outer world and found him in the form of Shams. Now the boundaries of 'I' and 'you' that marked Jalal and Shams had been destroyed, he knew that Shams was none other than himself. Jalal was God in the guise of an imam. Shams was God in the guise of a dervish. He and Shams were one and the same, just as he was one with the shepherd, and the shepherd's wife, the goat, the table, the fire. Everything that had ever existed was here and now. Shams was here, God was here.

Even as he bathed in the sudden light of grace, Jalal knew that this happiness would pass; he knew too that seeking to maintain this state would hasten its end, that only by letting go of God could he keep Him. If he wanted to walk with God, he would have to move continuously, and sometimes that would mean losing Him. And yet Jalal knew that even if desolation was felt again, that the absence from God was not real, that *all* was God – even the desolation, the loneliness, the nostalgia. Within every cry Jalal raised to the heavens of 'God, where are you?' had been hidden God's answer: 'Here I am.' And so it would always be.

•◆•

That night, while Jalal slept in the shepherd's hut, Shams came to him in a dream. 'I have forgiven Alaeddin,' he said. 'Now you, too, must forgive him. There is no room for ill will.'

When Jalal woke in the morning it was as though he was coming awake in the arms of his mother. So at peace, so well loved. He stretched his arms above his head, glad for once to be in this body, and then lay on the scattered straw and gazed up at the threads of light streaming through gaps in the roof. He was alone, and he realized he had slept long into the morning. A cockerel crowed from nearby: *'Allah-hu Akbar, Allah-hu Akbar!'* God is most great. Jalal smiled. Yes, yes.

The fluttering of a bird caught his attention as it landed on the thatched roof, and he idly followed its journey above him, guided by the rustling of palm leaves. It was a dove, and it cooed as though in response to the cockerel: *'Hu,'* it called. *'Hu.'* God, God.

The kid bleated outside the door: *'Bismillah!'* In the name of God. Jalal laughed like a child. The animals were doing *zikr*, the practice of remembrance of God. The whole of creation was giving thanks.

As he listened, he realized he had already forgiven his son Alaeddin. For it was not Alaeddin who had killed Shams. The knife had used the killer and not the other way. Shams had exposed his throat to his executioners and taunted them until they drew back the blade. If Alaeddin had not killed Shams, Jalal would have had to kill him with his own hands, for only by being forced apart from the friend could the final burning take place. Only when the final burning had happened, would the obstacle of the self be removed. Suddenly Jalal was flooded with gratitude towards his friend, a friend who had sacrificed his own life to save his own.

Jalal prayed for the soul of his son, the son who was the cause of the deliverance of the father. He prayed too for the soul of Shams, the man who had given him everything.

Jalal also saw that the life of Shams was not a gift for him alone, likewise the lives of Baha Walad and Seyyid Burhan. These teachers were not interested in a single man: their duty was to humankind. They were working to provide a gift to the world: the realized soul of Jalal. For *this* was the fulfilment of the fellowship with Shams: not the weeping of a bereft lover, not the howling lust for companionship, not the God-intoxicated madman, but a simple dervish, a servant on the path of love, outwardly sober and inwardly drunk.

The lyric poet had died, the seeker, the eloquent orator – they had all gone. Now a new Jalal was here, a man from whom personal desire had been burnt. Jalal no longer existed: he was the ears of everyone who listened, the heart of all who yearned. 'Remain silent as long as you desire to teach,' Shams had once told him. 'When the desire goes, *then* the ministry begins.' Jalal had arrived in Damascus as a slave, bound to the illusion of his separation to Shams; now he would leave as a servant: free and committed to the service of all who asked.

Come, come, whoever you are.

There was a knock at the door and it creaked open. A silhouette of a man was framed in the doorway. 'Ah! You are here, father.' It was Sultan Walad, the shepherd beside him.

Jalal rose and thanked the shepherd for his hospitality. The simple man touched the knees of Jalal and bade him farewell.

Jalal had come here, to this anonymous door in Damascus, dressed in rags, ashes in his mouth and found his God living inside. He knew then that at whatever door he knocked, in whatever strange town, he would find God there, for the door was that of his heart, and God lived within.

Sometimes I wonder, sweetest love
if you were just a dream
on a long winter night,
a dream of wine that fills the drunken eye.

Sometimes I wonder, sweetest love
if I should drink this ruby wine,
or rather weep: each tear a gem

with your face engraved,
a rosary to memorize your name.

There are so many ways to call you back.
Yes, even if you were just a dream.

END

Glossary

Allahu akbar: 'God is most great'
ayat: a verse from the Qur'an
azan: the call to prayer
dervish: a member of a fraternity of Sufis
djinn: a spirit which can take any form, and influence people by supernatural means
effendi: a term of respect, 'sir'
eid ul-fitr: the feast which marks the end of Ramadan
emir: a commander or governor
fakir: a mendicant dervish
fatwa: a formal legal opinion given by a mufti
hadith: traditions from the Prophet
hafiz: a person who has memorized the entire Qur'an
Hazreti: a title of respect for saintly persons
imam: a religious leader chosen by the community
insh'allah: 'God willing'
kaaba: the stone cube in Mecca towards which Muslims face when praying
kahin: a soothsayer of the pagan Arabs

kudum: a small double drum, played with sticks
kulah: a conical felt hat
La ilaha il al-Lah: 'There is no God but God'
maghrib: the fourth of the five Muslim prayers of the day, held just before sunset
malamati: a member of a Sufi tradition which considers that all outward signs of piety or religiosity are ostentations, and therefore take on despised work, do not pray or dress in clerical robes or advertize their poverty
mas'allah: 'What God does, is well done'
medrese: religious college
Mevlana: a title of honour, 'Our Master'
mimbar: the pulpit in a mosque
muezzin: the one who calls to prayer
mufti: a person who gives an opinion on a point of law
murid: a novice on the spiritual path
ney: a rim-blown bamboo flute
oud: a lute with six pairs of strings and played with a pick
Pir: literally, an elder
qalandar: an itinerant dervish who cares little for the externals of Islam
rebap: a two-stringed violin
Ramadan: the month of fasting
sema: the whirling devotional movement associated with the Mevlevi order
shariah: Islamic law

sheikh: the master of an order of dervishes
sunnah: according to the custom of the Prophet Muhammad
tekiya: a building for the training of dervishes
zikr: remembering God through invocation of God's names